Vahid rubbed at scrutiny of the lamplight below waver. The monster trembled with some unarticulated frustration. He sensed it. It manifested in the slight twitches to Erik's hand. That letter made matters worse—far worse. He cursed himself for delivering it.

"Do you have any idea what risk you put your children in? You made the choice to put them first when you took them out of the security of that monastery. You can't run off half-crazed right now."

Erik touched his temple. He leaned in slightly. "I *am* half-crazed. What would you suggest I do?" With one graceful leap he pounced upon the railing and began to walk, stabbing the air with a finger. "My fuse is smoldering and every minute that passes without her is a minute of absolute agony. I am growing angry, Daroga."

"You're not in the position you used to be—"

"Daroga—"

"You go running out onto those streets right now after her and you are as good as dead!" Vahid uneasily eyed Erik's twitching hand. "There is not a shadow in this city that doesn't know the Phantom, regardless of this fair. You have children here to think of and clearly your state of mind can't handle a thing right now." His eyes shot from Erik's hand, to his mask and back to his hand. Erik balanced precariously on the edge of the rooftop. The wind snapped his cloak sending arrows of tension up Vahid's neck.

And the raven, never flitting, still is sitting, still is sitting, On the pallid bust of Pallas just above my chamber door; And his eyes have all the seeming of a demon's that is dreaming...

He swallowed hard. "You stay here. I will return to the comte and attempt to leave with Anna." Erik's eyes shifted abruptly, moved, and glowed at him from an even higher spot. Vahid spun, searching high and low for his evaporating specter. "I will Erik. When have I ever backed down on my word to you? You can't have the control when you are the one out of it. Don't do anything stupid. Do you hear me, Erik? Stay burrowed like the mole you are until I come to you to let you know all is clear. You have children to consider, you colossal fool!"

A disembodied voice filled with all the surge of a rising tide and floated menacingly around him.

"Get off my roof, Daroga."

Rondeau

A Sequel to Madrigal:
A Novel of Gaston LeRoux's
The Phantom of the Opera

Jennifer Linforth

~~~

Highland Press Publishing
Florida

Rondeau

An Original Publication of
Highland Press Publishing - 2011

Copyright ©2011 Jennifer Linforth

Cover Copyright 2011 © Ken Altobello
Cover Concept – Hannah Phillips

For information, please contact
Highland Press Publishing,
PO Box 2292, High Springs, FL 32655.
www.highlandpress.org

ISBN: 978-0-9833960-8-6

HIGHLAND PRESS PUBLISHING

Excalibur Imprint

Dedication:

For my mother, Kathy, who I believe is the true meaning of heroine...

Acknowledgments:

I again thank critique partner Nina Pierce for her assistance in the writing of this chapter of The Madrigals. From marathon brainstorming sessions to her frank assessment of my work, she has been and continual source of insight and support.

Once again, thanks go to my editors for their work on this series. Thanks as well to Hannah Philips and Ken Altobello in the design of the cover.

To my comte and best friend I owe more than there are words in the world. His undying belief and support of me, from writing and beyond, is not only a gift and blessing but a rare and invaluable treasure. From my career as a writer to who am, I thank him with all my heart for everything. May God continue to bless us as best friends in every way. Toujours, croyez.

And finally my husband, Tony, has endless thanks for giving me the time away from family to finish this book. The dedication involved in writing is never easy, and his understanding though this journey I can't repay. Writing a book not only involves the author, but the entire family and such encouragement to keep going means much to me. I hold close how he cheers me on and strive to make him proud.

With memory set smarting like a reopened wound, a man's past is not simply a dead history, an outworn preparation of the present: it is not a repented error shaken loose from life: it is a still quivering part of himself, bringing shudders and bitter flavours and the tinglings of a merited shame
—George Eliot

Chapter One

It was his birthday, and the Vicomte de Chagny was thinking of ways to kill himself.

The toast ended. He raised his glass in acknowledgement, for just a second, before wanting to rip the lingering hurrahs out of his ears. Music resumed and men in formal black trousers, waistcoats, and white ties took to swirling white clad maids across the highly polished marble. Not that he cared. Eyes pulled so wide he swore they would crack, André Thaddeus Marie, Vicomte de Chagny regarded in stupid horror the surreal man plundering his way across the room.

His hand tightened around the champagne flute. He eyed the mantle to his side. One slight rap would be all it would take. He could shatter the flute and thrust the makeshift blade dead center of his chest. Death could be swift and he would not have to face what was inevitably about to ruin his sixteenth birthday. The man locked sights on him, instantly moistening André's brow. This was a sick champagne-induced hallucination! He turned to the circle gathering around him.

"So are we to assume music is in your future, André?"

André smiled at his godfather, Jules Legard. He flicked his eyes around the room before replying. Legard didn't seem concerned and he was head of Chagny security. His godfather's question was lighthearted. This was good though. He hadn't noticed anything was amiss. Life could move on as normal for a few more seconds.

"I'm afraid I don't understand music." André forced charisma to shine like the diamonds in his cuffs. He'd learned that trick from his diva mother. Always remain calm when eyes were upon you. But where did those eyes go? A bead of sweat trickled down the back of his neck. It felt like an invisible spider he couldn't crush. The massive mirrored wall to his side reflected the room. He searched it. Nothing seemed off... He turned from his reflection and despite his ill ease, nodded kindly at a blushing young maiden making doe eyes in his direction. *That* he learned from his father. Raoul Jean-Paul Marie the Comte de Chagny, charmed the ladies and always permitted them time—even if a serpent was poised to strike.

"What cares have I for music?" His laugh was rusty. "Notes are like thousands of annoying ants tromping off to ruin a picnic." Gesturing with his drink, he pointed one finger sharply at his godfather. "Don't you dare say I take after my mother."

"You should watch your tongue, Vicomte de Chagny, lest I make you prove what an accomplished baritone you truly are."

With a quick survey of the room to judge how much time he had before hell cracked open, André flashed a smile at his mother's response then dropped it like lead. She lifted her glass in toast before offering him a peck on his cheek. She left him alone on her bell-like laughter with the men gathered round him.

Thank God she headed in the opposite direction. No need for her to witness them all burning alive.

"He has a double first in mathematics and classics, Jules. I dare say if he continues this strong he can do whatever he wishes."

André rocked forward as his father's hand slapped his back as hard as his praise did. "While seeing the World's Fair has been a delight, all I wish is to leave Paris and return to Chagny in time to mount my stallion for the hunting season."

A voice slid over his shoulder from behind. "There are finer things to mount in life, Monsieur le Vicomte. But then again rumor has it you've already mastered the art of dipping your swell into fine young maids. I am...oh so proud."

André's lips turned into a tight line. This was no hallucination. This was all out nightmare. He glanced between Legard and his father before inching around to face to the rough, travel haggard man. Locking his eyes back on his father,

André saw him clutch his champagne flute so tightly it was a miracle it didn't shatter. Legard's face was crimson.

"André, attend your mother." His father's voice was low. Too low.

Unwilling to protest and utterly shocked to be staring at Loup, André made a hasty retreat. Glancing over his shoulder, the champagne flute finally exploded as his father slammed it down on the sideboard.

"My library. Now," he demanded of the bounty hunter, shaking his hand free of champagne.

Swallowing hard, André watched them storm from the ballroom. He glared remorsefully at his flute. A birthday death would have been much better than this.

* * * *

The strains of the latest waltz swirled in the distance, but Raoul focused on the fury rushing blood into his ears. Pacing around the library, he made several passes before stopping to glare out the floor to ceiling window. The reflection starring back at him, dim and ghost-like in the glass served him an extra dose of anger. Behind him Loup reclined casually on a settee, an arm slung over its back, the champagne flute he found gradually being drained.

"A year." Raoul spun from the reflection, disgust resonating in his voice. "I don't hear from you in a year and now you show up unannounced at my son's celebration?"

"How sweet. You missed me." Loup quaffed his champagne and propped a muddy boot on the seat.

Raoul strode across the room. He was usually a passive man but he allowed himself to feel his anger to the fullest.

You perpetual drunkard!

In one arch of his arm, Raoul ripped the glass from the man's grasp and flung it into the fireplace. The delicate crystal shattered, firing glass back at his feet.

Loup narrowed his eyes. "Temper, temper."

"Have you forgotten how to send word?" Legard interrupted.

Raoul eyed his man before scrubbing his face to hide his disbelief. He rammed a finger beneath this tie and yanked sharply. The bow fell free but did nothing to loosen the invisible noose around his neck. Minutes ago he was enjoying a delightful evening, now the past stalked him like a hungry lioness. "Where the hell have you been?" he interjected sharply.

Loup drew a line between the two of them with his eyes then studied his cuticles. "Sightseeing. I spent some time in a room with high security."

"You were in prison?" Legard yelled, arms akimbo.

"Where do you think I've been?" Loup stood, more pompous than a king at court. "You can stand here and look stupid or I can tell you what I know and leave you to your petty evening."

The tension was drawn as tight as a bowstring and, before it snapped, Raoul glanced to Legard. He jerked one hand to the ceiling and let it slap to his side. This would prove an interesting tale.

"Germany," Loup continued. "I had a mighty fine tryst with a Baron's daughter. Devilish shag that one."

Acid inched farther up Raoul's throat.

"After her father threw me in prison, I learned of monastery he was fond of in a tiny village. I decided to cut my sentence short and pay the village a visit. I was going to burn the church as a thank you for the kind accommodation he paid me over the last year, but the organ, you see, was far too extraordinary."

"If you so much as laid hand on a house of God—" Raoul pinched the bridge of his nose.

"Very interesting carvings on the organ cabinet. The dome of the Opera Garnier and the blackened masks caught my eye."

"What are you telling me?"

"I believe The Phantom of the Opera is sequestered near a monastery in Baden-Württemburg Germany close to the Austrian border."

Jutting a hip, Raoul sorted through a full year of information. Perplexed, he shook his head. "Baden-Württemburg? Last The Persian indicated, we should keep to the Royal Opera in Sweden. The Phantom was likely there."

"Yes, and the opera house in Salzburg, Rome, Barcelona, Copenhagen…" Loup dragged air over his tongue in a sound of disgust. "Your opera houses are dead ends and your Persian as helpful as gout. He's in Germany I assure you."

"But you said you believe?" Legard interrupted. "You're uncertain?"

The bounty hunter shrugged.

Raoul plowed a hand through his hair. He grabbed a clump as if to dig into his brain. He sat behind the desk and dropped his hands before his face like a prayerful priest.

For years I've pursued Erik for the crimes he committed at the Opera Garnier. Endless, hellish years of watching Christine vacillate between supporting locking the Phantom away forever and her steadfast devotion to her former tutor. Her Angel of Music! Now, it could be all at its end. "We should check with the Persian again before moving this to Germany."

"Oh bloody hell, you are a blithering imbecile!" Loup shouted. "That Persian is leading you in circles on purpose. His dark ass would be twitching at the opposite end of a guillotine if left up to me. Any fool can see he has some allegiance to your Phantom. I'm getting a delightful trek around the world on your purse string, but it's not challenging." He rapped his head with a finger. The motion made it seem like his beady eyes spun in their sockets. "You must think like a fugitive, not a gentleman. You should know by now opera houses are dead ends."

"I'm not about to upend innocent villages nor disturb a monastery without absolute confirmation the Phantom is there," Raoul said softly.

"All well and good, but I am not about to do a damn thing without my pocket padded. Where's my money?"

Raoul hardened his eyes. "You disappear for a year, challenge who I elect to question, and you have the audacity to demand my purse?"

"That was the arrangement. I don't hunt for free."

"The arrangement included proof." Raoul's shout bounced off the mosaic floor, nearly cracking the tiles. "You're not getting a dime from me. God's blood, you can't even bring in Anna Barret!"

The way Loup's tongue flicked out at the mention of Erik's companion tightened Raoul's neck. Loup pressed his hands against the worn wood of the desk and leaned in close. The man's breath was a vile as his morals. It curled Raoul's lip.

"It is your unfortunate luck Anna was involved in assisting the Phantom escape his crimes, Monsieur le Comte. She is a cunning little wench, but I'll find her." Loup laughed, making his stench more prevalent. "Anna's capture for the murder of that Duke's heir is gold. Only word of her death may stem the search in the good Duke's eye, but she is *my* commodity and I want her. I don't see you growing a spine to track them. Frankly, I don't see you doing much of anything requiring backbone." Loup's head lolled to the side with a droll expression as he regarded Raoul. He lifted a hand and rippled his fingers toward his palm. "Coat my hand and I will be on my way. I am mostly positive they are in Baden."

"Mostly is not good enough."

"Monsieur le Comte is correct," Legard agreed. "I'll not have Chagny involved in disrupting the peace. We need proof."

Loup shoved off the desk. "What proof do you need? I saw the organ. The village was as poor as they come. Where would they get one if not built at the hands of your musical genius? Why would monks give a fig about Parisian opera?"

"That Baron held it in esteem; he could have gifted the organ. And I've known several Brothers with talent at their hands," Raoul said.

"Talented enough to decorate it with *black* masks? I don't recall any being mentioned in the bible. God, you are pathetically stupid."

"If you are so certain he was in the village, then why didn't you bring him here?" Legard challenged.

Loup smiled like a cat with a canary in his throat. "I had to make a hasty retreat. Seems a prayer candle tipped over—"

"*For the love of God*! You burned down a monastery's church?" Raoul dug into the top of his head again, certain strands of hair broke off in his grip. His voice lifted. "I'll make amends to the village later, as soon as we have the Phantom in our grasp. I simply can't think of that now. Erik is living a normal life in the German countryside as if he never abducted Christine, never killed the managers of the Garnier, and never burned down a carriage house! How dare he! How dare that man live without a conscience!" His fist hit his desk turning his signet into a gavel. "After all he did to Paris and Christine.

After killing *my brother...*" Raoul glanced from Loup to Legard.

"We need to know for certain if he would be in Germany. Go to the Rue de Rivoli. Wake the Persian if you must. This can't wait. Ask him directly of these opera houses. If anyone knows Erik's wandering ways it is he." Legard nodded while Loup rolled his eyes. Raoul jerked his head in his direction. "If you have better means to back up your suspicions then speak them now." He spoke to Legard again. "Find out what you can, then you,"—he pinned Loup with his look—"will return to Germany and not return without an end to this manhunt."

* * * *

Spit slid down the wood. Loup watched it slime the library door he just exited thinking he had better things to make wet than polished wood. The comte dare shout orders at him? Chagny owed him money and he knew exactly where to get it. It would just be a matter of finding her alone. His gut had a need for liquor and his loins a wild release. It trumped any necessity to locate the Comtess de Chagny and her purse, but to his good fortune he didn't have to. The beauty rounded the corner. Her delicate hand fluttered at the base of her throat as she regarded the floor. Wiping the spittle from his lips, Loup pressed a long leg against a marbled column.

"Comtess de Chagny. Miss me?" Like a deer before the bow of a hunter, she froze. He sneered. "Come now. Don't look so shocked. You knew I would return. We have a deal, remember?"

All good humor faded from her face. Her porcelain skin blanched. Fine lines marched across its flawless perfection, aging her instantly.

"What are you doing here?" she gasped. "You've not found Erik, have you?"

"I might have. Your husband is eager to coat my palms to bring him in, but reluctant to pay me. One of you must or someone will not be happy."

Loup pushed off the column and swaggered toward her. The comtess was always a meek thing before him, the perfect toy to which to amuse himself until he had Anna back in his grip. Nothing compared to that feisty chit. His skills as a hunter were unrivaled. He always got what he wanted in the blink of an eye—except Anna. The blasted woman had become his prize game—and the idea of giving up his favorite bauble to anyone else raised his temper. He would prevail over them all somehow and savor every moment of victory while his hands were coated with money, and his swell with Anna's body.

He trailed a gritty finger down Christine's elegant arm and walked behind her, admiring her shape and size with roaming hands.

"It would be amusing to see what would happen if I spilled that secret I've been keeping all these years of your love for the Phantom. It might be more fun than the money you are paying me to keep silent about it. The scandal would level Chagny to rubble. Your son would lose so much, now, wouldn't he?" Loup rested his chin on her shoulder and wiggled his palms before her eyes. "I believe I know where Erik is and your husband is desperate for him. If you still want me to keep your marriage the happy little lie it is—pay up!"

Loup snatched her earlobe with his teeth and nipped sharply. A lewd chuckle grew deep in his throat as his tongue circled her neck. He loved when women trembled. "You know how to fill my bags with the money."

Lightly pushing her away, Loup spun on his heel and headed down the hall, his hands dangling before him like a puppeteer working the strings of a marionette. The gentle tune of *Alouette* fell from his lips and skipped beside him down the corridor.

* * * *

Christine refused to turn until that tune faded. Her worst nightmare danced in the hall of her home and it made the air around her seem icy. Her heartbeat ticked fearfully making it near impossible to catch her breath. When she did turn, a gasp leapt from her mouth.

"André, I didn't see you." She looked beyond him. Loup had disappeared. It was little comfort.

"I didn't mean to startle you, *Maman.*"

Christine smoothed the lines of her gown and pinked her cheeks with her hands. Years of stage training came into play as she covered her nerves flawlessly. "All is well, André. I was merely seeking your father. Return to your party. We'll speak later."

Her son didn't move. A knot tightened in her throat as she watched him extend a leg and jut his hip. *So like his father...*

"Why is Loup here? He usually surfaces like a bad potato, but he's been gone for quite some time. I thought perhaps for good at last. That man's despicable behavior and morals is not something I appreciate associated with my family—despite Father's desires. Does he have word on the Phantom and Mademoiselle Barret?"

The hall might as well have been a stage, but her the only actor. André had a knack for speaking his mind as he saw fit. She had to give her best performance yet. She tapped her son's arm.

"I have no idea why he has returned. I will speak to your father of it, André," Christine placated. "Go, return to your guests."

She kissed him on his cheek hoping the icy sensation she felt inside didn't make her lips as cold and betray her to her son. Hastening past him and the library door, she forgot all about Raoul. Air is what she needed and this time she dared not turn around lest her son read the cheat on her face.

Chapter Two

He read the same sentence four times. Glancing over its rim, his book fell lax between two fingers. Paris was supposed to equal solitude and culture for him. All were currently being disrupted as the pounding persisted. Slapping his book aside Vahid scowled toward the door, wondering who would disturb him at such an unheard of hour.

"I'm coming. There is little need to break down my door!"

The rapping continued, raising his ire with every step his feet made across his elaborate Persian carpet. As the former Daroga, chief of police to Persia's Sultana years ago, privacy was a luxury he came to enjoy, having had little of it. Being disturbed regardless of the hour wasn't something he found pleasant and he was certain it wasn't a harem of fine virgins pounding their way into his apartments. Yanking open the door, the face greeting him instantly skewed his brow.

"For all Allah has in Paradise, what do *you* want?"

"Daroga, may I have a word?" Legard politely bowed and removed his hat.

"No you may not. Go away." Leaning all his weight against the door, Vahid attempted to shut it.

His uninvited guest shoved a boot between the jambs and forced his way into the modest flat. He peeled off his gloves and placed them inside his hat. "You're not going to offer me a drink?"

"I have hemlock."

Legard smiled. It was wry, skewing Vahid's face even more. He knew the reasons the former Paris investigator was here. It made him wish to combust like the strike of a match. "Inspector, leave my home. You're not welcome here."

"When I'm on business my position is welcome anywhere. You should know that."

A sound of utter disgust burst out his lips. It was pointless to argue; after all, he was already in his apartment. Vahid searched the room. *Where did I leave my drink?*

"Tell me, Daroga,"—Legard helped himself to a seat in an overstuffed chair—"these opera houses you keep suggesting... Any others you might have in mind? Hamburg perhaps? Shall we look for him there?"

Him. Vahid stopped mid-search. *There it is again. The reason for these blasted unannounced meetings.* The Daroga found his aperitif on the sideboard and downed a massive gulp. He pressed a finger to the center of his chest and the burn sliding down his throat. He was getting too old for this. Legard had become his own private Phantom, popping in and out of his life when Chagny needed information or hit a wall. He cursed himself under his breath. He never should have allowed Chagny to question him years ago to begin with. Blissful ignorance should have been the way to go so he could have carried on with his life and not permitted his foolish curiosity over Erik to resurface.

"Do you have anything to say to me, Daroga?

"Let me think a moment. Yes...go away."

"You know you can't hinder an investigation you are involved in."

His drink splashed over the rim of his glass to coat his hand as he spat his second swig out. "Involved in? I have nothing to do with this! Deal with your own investigation, you incompetent, measly, old fool and leave me out of it."

"You *are* involved. We expect you to be—"

"—the eyes and ears for Chagny. Well aware, Monsieur. I suddenly feel blind and deaf in my old age."

The liquor churned within him along with the reality that keeping Erik out of his life was an impossibility. He, unlike most, had known his secrets for years. Wiping his drink off of his wrist, he looked at Legard. Just the sight of him made his nostrils flare. Vahid was aware Erik had faked his death years ago and never killed Philippe de Chagny.

Erik may have attempted to kill the former comte in the distant past, Monsieur, but his ultimate demise was not at the monster's hands. There is no proof! Regardless, I've made it a point to stay away from him when he did resurrect himself. I don't know where Erik is! Logic would deem the monster would hide in the bowels of theaters like he always did. History tends to repeat, after all. Far be it from me to inform Chagny that the entire idea of Erik's faked death was Philippe de Chagny's to begin with.

Vahid swallowed a snort and refilled his glass. Maybe it would drown his thoughts. "Why you keep pestering me I'll never know. Not once...once," he shouted, "has Erik made contact with me. Yet here you are at my door again like a dog sniffing for a bone."

He shook his head as if to rattle the entire affair back into its proper place. Back then Erik's temper was explosive. Shamed and shunned in the most humiliating ways caused his old comrade to be unpredictable and the Daroga had wanted nothing to do with him. Swore Erik out of his life forever, but unfortunately he was a weak man. At least when it came to the deep ties he had to Erik.

Not this time. He was through.

Tossing the drink on top of the sideboard so suddenly it wobbled and spun, he headed for the door and yanked it open. "Get out. I'll answer no more of your questions."

"Germany, Daroga. Don't make me arrest you."

The door slammed. "Fine! Germany! Hell no! For the last and final time I'll tell you, not a chance."

Legard rose and snatched his hat, shoving it between them angrily. "Then sending Loup back there to uncover what he found in a *monastery* in Baden-Württemburg is useless? It appears your opera houses are wild chases Daroga!" He escalated the conversation to a shouting match. "By God, help us don't hinder us. The evidence is there. If Germany comes up empty then where do you suggest we look? And no opera houses. I grow weary of this game—"

"He would not be in Germany. He hates Germany. Always had. When will that get through to you?"

"Then *where*, Daroga? You know him better than most."

"Perhaps up your ass?"

A chilling silence followed the stalemate. "Thank you for your time, Daroga. As always, it was charming."

"Go drink from the river."

Tipping his hat, Legard stepped through the door that was being impatiently held open. "Delightful to see you again, too. Should you remember anything or decide you have information to assist us—"

"I will be certain to jump naked into a scorpion's nest." The door slammed hard in Legard's face.

Once the crack stopped echoing in his apartment, Vahid sank into his armchair, sullen and bitter that a lovely evening had to end this way. There would be no finishing that book now. Glancing out the window, he watched Legard mount his horse, and ride off toward the Tuileries.

Chagny is absolutely obsessed! When will they learn I am not going to give them an ounce of information even if I had it? If they poured half their efforts into mopping up the crime riddling Paris, the streets would be so clean one could eat off of them.

"Germany. Why would he be in Germany?"

His brooding matched the falling night. Once Erik influenced one's life he remained an all too vivid part of it. The stories he had heard about him rolled about in his head. But were they really stories, or more rumor and legend? Erik was all too real to Raoul de Chagny, that much was certain. The Daroga sniffed his glass. All too real to him as well. He hadn't set eyes on Erik in years. The tales he spun recalled a broken man, reclusive and scorned, wallowing in solitude beneath an Opera House convinced the world would love without him.

Erik murdered again. That was one tale he couldn't ignore. The monster's deadly past, prevalent in Persia, seemed to haunt him still. Yet a paid political assassin was different. Or was it? Vahid took a deep breath. Erik could have been such a different man, capable of such glory and good. If only he had never laid eyes on Christine Daaé. Then he would never have known how much it could hurt to love and none of this would have ever happened.

Staring out the window only reflected his somber mood back at him. He knew sides of Erik no one else did. The side capable of being a great man with great love. He couldn't believe the images painted for him by this pursuit. He tried desperately to put the thoughts out of his head, but he couldn't help but wonder about a long lost chapter in his life.

"Baden-Württtenburg," he whispered into his drink.

Chapter Three

The ice on the window glinted in the early dawn light blinding him to seeing anything but brilliant white. Erik stared toward the church through the frosted window of the monastery's eastern wing.

Charred wood had been hauled away and fire scarred stones cleansed, but still the stench of acrid smoke lingered in the air. It would be months until the pillar of the village rose again to shelter its flock. For now, the monastery's church wafted its untimely fate on a gentle breeze and the persistent scent crept through a crack in the pane. Clasping his hands behind his back Erik mused nothing in life was simple, least of all the unresolved mystery of why fire would ever touch such an innocent place. Not to mention why a man such as him—a certain sinner—would be forgiven his past and given a peaceful, nondescript life in a German monastery.

"For someone who is not a man of God you certainly have been down to the church more in these last few weeks than in all the years I have known you."

Erik turned. Through the depth of his mask he coolly regarded Brother Lukas.

"Should you not be in private prayer before Lauds instead of bothering me?" Erik preferred to dismiss socializing. He was content with the same eerie solitude that had always been his companion. "Being your personal cause for redemption is getting stale." He lifted a brow the monk couldn't see. The only thing he could see was the curl to his lip that betrayed his jest.

"Personal causes are not old. You are. You shouldn't be sulking over a lost organ. Accidents happen by God's design."

"I never believed in your God and I dare say I am a better designer."

He turned toward the frosted window. The ice crystals shook in the light. A master architect in addition to a brilliant

Maestro, Erik crafted his way through this new, quiet life of his. Brother Lukas spent his afternoons in the carpentry shop, silently praying and tending to repairs for the monastery and church—until Erik arrived and took over, insisting not even Christ was a better carpenter then he. The monk chuckled, prompting a smile to creep across Erik's lips.

"Erik doesn't sulk, he broods," Anna replied.

Erik looked across the modest kitchen and cocked his head at the petite woman seeing to his morning meal. The dawn attempting to peer through the window caught her hair, making it glimmer like a copper kettle peppered silver. The light trapped there drew him from the window like a macabre hummingbird to nectar. He slid behind her, walking his extraordinarily long fingers up her spine. The mask spared the world all but his lips, allowing him to gently touch that spot on her neck he knew always made her knees soften.

"You may brood over a lost organ yet one side of you certainly has no problems being inspired." The Brother tilted his head in Erik's direction.

"Consider it the least your fine God could do for me." Erik passed a hand over his mask. "I would offer to teach you the art of seduction, but I feel it would be lost on you."

"The art of seduction?" A cold blast of air swirled through a side door and around the grinning youth in the doorway. He rippled his fingers through his hair building upon his roguish appearance before leaning his elbow on the doorframe. He shrugged his eyebrows. "Don't stop such conversation on my behalf. I assure you my curiosity is peaked."

Erik glowered. "Philippe, it is an ungodly hour. You never rise early. What are you doing roaming about?"

His son folded his arms and ambled into the kitchen. Unusually tall for fifteen, he dwarfed his mother as he passed. He yanked at the strip of leather holding his shoulder length, brown hair in a neat queue, adjusted it, and tied it again. The brow he lifted accented eyes the color of a stormy Caribbean sea.

"I was looking for something." He rubbed the back of his neck.

"Looking for what?" Erik countered.

"Something I lost."

"Elaborate."

He didn't have to. The missing item tore through the door behind him, squealing gleefully at her freedom. The whorl of blonde curls burst into the kitchen, her laughs a vibrant upheaval to the peace of many a monk. Her bare feet and the hem of her nightdress were hopelessly covered in cobwebs and dust. The ever present violin and bow was, as usual, clutched tightly in one hand. No one understood why she carried the silent instrument; she had no knowledge of how to play it. It was her security and left unquestioned. Slamming a hug into Erik's leg, she tilted her head as far back as she could and flashed a mischievous grin. The pungent, mildewed aroma hovering around her, reminiscent of his years living in the cellars of the Opera Garnier, caused Erik to shoot a fiery look to his son.

"*Philippe Georges Marie.*" The protective growl grew deep in his throat. "Keep Simone in check!"

"She wasn't beside me when I woke." Philippe shrugged. "I found her in the catacombs sitting by Pappy's tomb rambling about singing horses and dancing dogs."

Beneath his mask, Erik's face heated to an uncomfortable level. If there was one place he didn't like his daughter playing it was in cellars. Keeping his past as The Phantom of the Opera hidden was already a challenge. He couldn't blame her for visiting with that old curmudgeon who had traveled with them year after year. Pappy had been as a grandfather to her.

Simone's cheeks plumped with her smile, softening the edges of his ire. It was capable, for now, of drawing the attention away from the bare ridges of bone and skull marring most of her face. Her voice was tinged with an unusually haunting timbre, its resonance defying her seven years.

"Papa, I have a flower for you." She thrust it toward his face.

Erik knelt. He brushed a wayward curl from her face and watched her eyes cross as it sprung back into shape. Simone's untamed hair cascaded down the length of her back, hiding some of her face from his view. It certainly hid her missing ear, but did nothing to conceal her absent nose or the paper-thin flesh stretching across three-quarters of her face. Small for her age, she had his looks, his voice and the amazing quality of his eyes. All he had to do was shift their position slightly into shadow and they would flash an eerie, yet captivating shade of gold. His fingers rippled across her deformity as if doing so would brush away the guilt he carried for creating that part of her. Little girls should look like angels, not bear the curse of a face of Death.

He took her gift, somewhat remorseful over the flower's untimely demise. Perhaps accepting it would lessen the blow of what he was about to tell her. Born without breath in her body until a dedicated doctor saved her life, her mind reacted unlike most children her age. "Simone," he explained gently as he rose, "horses cannot sing."

"Yes they can." The violin thumped against her thigh as she made a Maypole of his leg.

He looked to Anna. Laughing, she carried plates from the counter to the table and shared a moment with Brother Lukas. Both lifted their shoulders unwilling to touch such a statement. Simone was a mystery, a tiny enigma that had everyone wrapped neatly around her pinky.

"Horses sing *Alouette*," she insisted. "And dogs dance to it. They did so in the church before the spooky man lit it up with fire."

Plates crashed to the floor in a thunderous explosion circling a target of clay throughout the kitchen. Erik's eyes darted from his daughter's yelp to Anna's shaking hands in time to see the blood rush out of her face.

"Philippe, take your sister," he snapped. "Bathe her and get her a clean frock. I need to speak to your mother alone."

"I think not." Philippe's voice felled the room silent. "If Simone saw something—"

"Simone saw nothing," Brother Lukas quietly assured. "Children are to obey their elders, Philippe. Do as your father asks."

"We've been trying to uncover what happened to the church for weeks. Simone may not have seen anything, but she clearly heard something. It is obviously linked to my father's colored past, judging from Mother's reaction."

The air rushed around him as Erik pivoted to Philippe. His tall frame hunched immediately into his shock as he approached his son with an undisguised curiosity. For years he'd made it a point to keep all details of his past away from his children. Though he regretted ever telling the monk of his history, he knew the man of God would never betray him to his kin. Saving the village from illness years prior had been Erik's saving grace and security, yet his son spoke with the arrogance of a king, causing his eyes to narrow.

"My colored past?" He chanced a look to Anna. The ripple on her face deepened.

"You don't think I believe we wandered from vagabond camp to vagabond camp across France all those years because it was the life of comfort you so sought for your children?"

The corner of Erik's lip twitched as he tried to govern his shock.

"You will continue this conversation with me present," Philippe instructed. "It involves the church and clearly Chagny, as evidenced by the mention of *Alouette*." He made a casual gesture toward Simone who clung, perplexed, to Erik's leg.

The silence in the room could have made hair stand on end.

"Chagny?" Anna gasped incredulously. "What know you of Chagny?"

"I know enough. Any time men with rifles arrived at a camp we had to run. You and Father switched from German to speaking French. I caught on years ago there was something you didn't want us to know. Simone may not speak a lick of it, but I taught myself French quite easily. I'm fluent." Philippe spread his hands. "Surprise."

The only movement in the room was Simone as she made a fifth spin around her makeshift Maypole. The scrutiny of Philippe's unblinking eyes bore into Erik, yet he was too shocked to do anything other than listen in a dumbstruck and smoldering silence. The carefully constructed secrets of his past had suddenly cracked open out of the blue, spilling the letters of disaster at his feet.

"One of the armed gents, a bizarre, detached sort of fellow, always hummed *Alouette*." Philippe's causal comment sank Anna into a chair. "I've wondered about your secrets for too long. I understand more than your realize. The Brothers here have been my family. If I can help solve what happened to the church, I will."

"Someone remove my daughter from this room, immediately. I will not have her innocence manipulated. Clearly my son's already is."

"Stop mollycoddling her, Father, and cease treating me like an infant. Simone is not able to comprehend a word we're saying no matter the language we speak. You know how backward her mind is. If you're in trouble, I can help. I spent years without a home, listening to you whisper about Chagny. I'm not stupid. I could see the rifles as clearly as you could. This is my opportunity to *finally* know why."

"Philippe, I am warning you..."

"Warn me all you want. I demand to know."

That was his mother's ever-defiant spirit shining though and Erik would tolerate it from her but not him. Erik didn't think before the tone of his voice switched to one sharp as bell and hushed as a whisper, able to level the strongest of men into submission.

"Philippe, I am a simple carpenter. Play with your sister."

Philippe was unmoved. He looked at him in such a way Erik couldn't decipher his next move. His son's eyes darted from one parent to the other.

"The simple carpenter excuse again, Father? Is that to explain why you built a pipe organ in the first place and so painstakingly carved it? Explain why locked in a trunk in a secluded room of a monastery there's an opera cloak of the finest quality and a score written in your hand?"

Rubbing his mask, Erik slowly lowered his hands hoping to summon some form of calm. *How did he find that trunk*? "Are you going to continue this, Philippe?"

"Furthermore there is the matter of that violin Simone carts around." He gestured to the instrument still thumping against her thigh as she rounded her pole.

Large puffs of breath broke rhythmically through the nose Erik lacked. He extended a hand to Anna, silently asking *her* to keep him calm. He hadn't played his violin since before Philippe was born. A different time...a different place. It was a silent ghost of his past accidentally found and adopted by Simone. Playing, composing, and being one with the magic in his soul had been too risky on the run.

"No simple carpenter has a violin capable of making the music that one can," Philippe said wondrously. "It has a tone richer than the heavens themselves."

Those words formed a lasso and looped around Erik's neck. They yanked his face up to squarely regard his son. "How do you know what that sounds like?"

"I've played it on several occasions."

"*You have what?*" The walls nearly crumbled. His heart pounded in his ears and he couldn't tell if it was from fury or joy.

"I tried to teach myself with the score in that trunk. But music is difficult to understand. Every note is jumbled and looks backward." He tapped his temple giving his father the first indication of his frustration.

Breaking away from Anna and Simone prompted a worried glance from her and a scowl from his daughter. Philippe struck a chord and it was vibrating painfully through every bone in Erik's body. The exchange that happened next ran around the room like a mouse before a cat. There was no place to hide.

"You're not a simple carpenter, Father. With a voice as unique as yours, a score like no other, and the finest of violins? I've heard you and Mother speak of the Opera Garnier—"

"That cloak, the violin...they were all in this monastery when we arrived!"

"No they weren't."

"Philippe, I will not tell you again—"

"You're a Maestro aren't you?"

"*Philippe, I am warning you.*"

"From Paris."

"*Philippe—*"

"You had an ingénue..."

"*I am a carpenter! Now—*"

"You're that living myth, that murderer and Maestro, The *Phantom* of the *Opera!*"

Chapter Four

Unearthly stillness filled the room as if stolen from the bowels of the catacombs. Erik paced circles around the central table making the only noise, a soft swish of fabric against his legs. For once he was pleased a mask hid his expression.

Sliding his eyes from the pinched lips of the monk, he noticed Anna's face was so stiff a breeze could have shattered it. Simone had stopped in her tracks, her extraordinary eyes as large as a harvest moon. Philippe's hands had rolled into fists. Erik clamped down on his teeth until his ears rang.

"I will not be hunted!" *I would sooner die than be subjected to life as a mongrel on the run again.* Striding forward he stood eye to eye with his son. The black of his mask reflected in the flawless perfection of Philippe's eyes. "Can you handle what you want to know?"

Philippe nodded.

Erik backed away. It mattered not how he knew of The Phantom of the Opera. His legendary past had on more than one occasion been fodder for traveling minstrels. It was all he could do to keep his family out of sight and not dispatch every wandering troubadour he came across. What mattered was how one explains a past of murderous vengeance to a child. How to adequately explain the cancer of madness in a mind? The only answer he had lay in his daughter's hand.

She didn't speak as she looked up at him. His children knew there were times when best not to say a word. Erik walked beyond her. His son could handle what he needed to know—but could Simone? Control over his past had suddenly been yanked from his grasp, leaving him with little choice. Erik rounded. He took the violin, ignoring her heart stabbing cries of outrage. He brushed his thumb across the strings. Anyone who disturbed him would have done so at their own risk as he turned each peg and tuned the long neglected instrument back into life. He did so silently, every so often meeting the eyes locked on him. Simone's were the most intense. Erik turned his back to her and lifted the violin to his chin. He heard Anna's breath hitch. The bow hovered over the bridge. A bone rattling tremble for command over the noise inching into his mind started at his toes and would have vibrated his arm if he didn't fight it back. Noise...was his madness.

He wouldn't have it.

The violin became a virgin begging to be stroked, and his soul a man begging to tame her. He touched the bow to the bridge and coaxed the first agonizing notes from the instrument.

Liquid gold tones rose and fell on waves of ecstasy as his feelings transformed from his mind to music. Those in the room appeared to be filled with soundless wonder as he played. Chancing a look at Philippe, Erik's drunken eyes saw his hands relax. No longer clenched from tension, Philippe's elegant fingers took on a life of their own, undulating in tune to the music. There was a repressed Maestro in the boy. Erik felt it in his soul. The warmth he felt upon seeing Philippe evaporated to a deep and overwhelming sense of foreboding when he looked at Simone. The tiny scowl, as her eyes chased something invisible, he knew all too well. Within her mind was a private prison of euphoria only present when he composed his most fantastic pieces.

Shaken to the core by that haunting look, he nodded to Anna, cuing her to tell his story before his resolve crumbled. The pain in his chest broke out upon the strings as music carried her quavering words around the room.

"Philippe, to understand him, is to understand music..."

* * * *

Erik laid the violin on the table. The fingers on his bow arm tingled from overuse. Stretching his hand, he rubbed his upper arm, unconsciously kneading the ancient gunshot wound that caused them to prickle. Raoul de Chagny had even marred his abilities on the bow. Looking across the room, the lines of emotion on his son's face were unreadable. The meeting of their eyes caused Philippe to square his shoulders ramrod straight.

"I need air." He stormed toward the door, threw it open, and disappeared.

Tension was so thick the Brother's robes could have hung upon it. Erik paced, rubbing his hand. Any concern he had over the tone in Philippe's voice disappeared as a blonde devil leapt upon the bench at the table, stopping his heart dead.

"*Simone, nein!*"

Snatching back her beloved instrument, she strangled the violin with one tiny hand. Angry lines marched across her misshapen face, puckering her forehead and making her deformity a ghastly sight to behold. She peered under the bridge before ferociously shaking it.

"How did it make noise? Where did it come from? Inside? Do you keep the birds in it or in my head? How did you get them on the air?" The violin jabbed up and down in time with her frustration.

Anna crossed the room in a heartbeat, calmly trying to pry the priceless violin from her deathly grip. The girl grabbed the offending instrument to her chest.

"The bird flew away!" She stomped, rocking the bench as she shook the violin again. "Too much music! Always too many birds in my head and now they are in here? My birds went away, into here, and I want my birds back!"

Erik paused and for a second weighed her words with a leaded-hearted dread. Music and noise often combined in his mind like a cancerous cocktail resulting in years of madness. Never equating it to the likes of birds, he dismissed her comment as the ramblings of a disoriented little girl. Rubbing his temple, he groaned at the battle ensuing between mother and daughter for his beloved instrument. He couldn't look. Nothing survived Simone's curiosity and lest she snap it in two he finally cracked. "Let her have it! Just let her have it!"

Simone stomped from the bench to stand squarely on the table. Spoons scattered everywhere. Fist on one hip the other tucking the violin and bow under her arm like a brilliant concertmaster, she leaned as far forward as she dared and challenged Brother Lukas. "Make him tell me how he did that! Tell him to give me back my birds! They belong in here." She pointed to her head. "He cannot have my birds." Another foot hit the table. "*My* birds!"

"Simone, why don't you go outside and try to track down those missing birds?" Brother Lukas urged softly upon catching the warning look Erik sent his way. "See where they flew to and bring them back to the violin."

Simone jumped off the table and tramped out the door, shouting and pointing at her father with the bow as if it were a sword.

"The birds are mine!"

Dumbfounded silence filled the room as the swirl of curls disappeared out the door.

"All in all that was mild confrontation between Simone and a new situation," Brother Lukas observed. "Since you started this, you both had better be prepared to finish it."

"Why?" Erik whispered. "I spent a good portion of my life keeping secrets locked away. It makes things tidy."

"You've no choice now. They're going to question, and you better figure out the answers." He looked out the window toward Philippe. "That boy is going to want to know why his Maestro father has chosen to settle in an area like this, building an organ for monks and a God he has no faith in. You can't just tell them you were a reclusive Maestro at the Garnier. He will ask specifics about this manhunt, your asylum here, and more about the Phantom. I'll not even ponder what might be going on in the little one's mind." The monk nodded. "Does this have anything to do with who Simone saw?"

Rage rushed down Erik's spine. "I can fix an organ. I can design a church. I cannot fix the *innocence of my family!*" His shout echoed into the fireplace. "*The family I always wanted!*" Bracing his hands against the mantel, he clutched the wood until his skeletal knuckles turned whiter. Pure hatred poured out of his words and into the dancing flames. "Only one man I know sings that song."

"Loup," Anna whispered. Erik turned to look at her. She massaged a scar upon her temple, panic eddying her words. "We have to tell the children everything. If Chagny and Loup have found us here—then they need to know. Philippe will understand."

"Will he, Anna?" The question was loaded.

Anna dug at the wood of the table with a finger. Encouraged only by Brother Lukas' nod did she continue. "We answer whatever questions he has. He'll understand."

"And what of Simone?" Crossing his arms, Erik's defensiveness swelled to the surface. He lifted one gnarled finger in the direction of the monk, reminding him to mind his tongue. All the Brothers were protective of the child, but none more so than the one who shared her curse. "You are so confident the boy will understand what went on in that opera house? *Fine.* So he understands. Shall we take it a step further to before you arrived? Perhaps I confirm his suspicions of my great ingénue, sing him some tunes from those operas I taught Christine, fill him in on the chandelier that fell and the concierge I killed as a result, share my affinity for English sweets and a mindless box keeper, lay out the plans for him of my house deep below ground, and perhaps mention a torture chamber or two. Why not a scorpion or a grasshopper? Jolly high! Which will he turn? If he likes *that,* I can show him more than just my skills on a violin. Maybe he would enjoy the silk rope!" Erik's voice swelled.

"Better yet, let us go further! *Persia was an absolute delight!*" He punched the air with a fist. "Some of my finest work occurred before the Shah!" Palms to the table, he leaned in, searing Anna with his stare. "I am certain after that he would be so drunk with happiness he would be dying to know his father spent the better half of his boyhood as the alluring Living Corpse." The fingers on his hand sprung open as he yanked his mask from his face and thrust it across the room. "How wonderful it will be for him to know I traveled from flee ridden fair to flee ridden fair with my managers singing like a *damned deformed canary!*"

Erik cleared the contents from the top of the table with one violent swing of his arm. Bowls and spoons flew everywhere. Anna jumped. Brother Lukas extended a hand to her, waving his fingers for her to come to the comfort of his side.

Erik plucked at the flesh near his eyes as if his fingers were beaks pecking into his skull. "You have this belief that everyone will understand and accept as you do. Accepting me is not easy. Even for a genius like Philippe and a simple child like Simone. If we want the children to know, then *I* need to know. After all these years...why, Anna? Why has it been so easy for you to understand me?"

The silence pouring off of her body was an enemy not to be tested. She turned to the monk, but said not a word.

"I will mind the children." Brother Lukas was halfway out the door when Erik agreed.

"I think you should." Once alone, he stood like an unmoved mountain waiting indignantly for her response.

"Brussels," she replied.

"Lovely city, wonderful potatoes."

"I was sixteen, before I came to Paris and staying in Brussels with my father along with Laroque and Wischard."

His eyes pinched and he dropped his sarcasm. "I thought you did not know the managers of the Opera Garnier before your arrival at my Opera House."

"I lied. They were the great trio of Europe, running cons left and right through every major city they came across. I was the annoying little attachment that came with Barret. My job? Pick pockets mostly. I'm quite good at it." She leaned into him and mocked his previous soliloquy. "Perhaps I can teach it to Simone." Anna walked to the far side of the room, the hem of her skirts swishing angrily. "Pick the pockets when I was told, divert police when I was told, bed who I was told."

Erik tightened his jaw. He glanced out the window. The thought of her lying with any man roiled his blood.

"You want to know why I understand your life, Erik? Then look at me!"

Trepidation spread though his veins. Slowly looking over his shoulder, his gaze slid up her body until they locked with a fury behind her eyes. He wasn't certain he wanted her to continue.

"They gambled—a lot—and usually won. Until the night they met their match in Duke de Molyneux and his son. One particular evening, they lost. They were about to pay the money owed, when they had a wonderfully wicked idea. Trade me instead. The duke's heir was a strapping young man, had everything in his life handed to him on a silver platter. Imagine my shock when I was on that platter. I was upstairs sleeping in a small corner of the floor reserved for the dog and me when the games began. It's a lovely feeling to be gambled away to a spoiled boy for his adolescent need for pleasure. I fought him with everything I had, until the duke thought it might be fun to join his son."

The usual soft German lilt to Anna's voice turned uncharacteristic, unnerving him. He retrieved his mask and replaced it on his face. Perhaps it would shield him from her words. "Anna, stop," he pleaded.

"Two men, *at the same time* taking what they wanted, laughing and raping me, while my father stayed downstairs smoking a cigar—"

"Stop, now."

"Do you know what I did, Erik?"

"Anna, please—"

"I was streetwise by that time and smart enough to hide a knife within my reach. The boy was easy. He was my size. But the duke...*took a few tries.*"

"*Cease.*"

"I eventually gave up, he was too strong. But I at least had the chance to run. The duke should have considered himself lucky the chest wall is a difficult thing to puncture for a girl of my size."

"*Anna.*"

"I understand because I tasted it. I know what it's like. The sudden surge of control and power as if you are the Supreme Being able to defend against any who hurt you. Murder can feel good." She twisted her way across the room avoiding Erik's attempts at reaching her. "Until it sinks in and you run. I ran as far as I could get, my father chasing me through alleyways until that crossroad by a Brussels street. He caught up to me. I still had the knife, and I used it again. But the one man I wanted to kill so badly, I couldn't. So I ran into that crowd and never stopped." Anna backed herself toward the door. "Every waking minute I spend wondering how my hands could have killed a boy my own age. Praying somehow I can forgive myself. Praying every morning that I can look my son in the eyes and not see the boy's face. Wondering what it will be like when Philippe turns seventeen knowing there was one boy who didn't! Pondering how to turn back time knowing since the day Philippe was born he has been hunted by the same huntsman whose sworn duty was to find me. I'm *Alouette*,

Erik! I'm the lark Loup wants to skin. He's only connected to Chagny because he wants me—and I'm with you."

"Anna—"

"*Leave me alone!*" She flung Erik's arm aside as he reached for her. Before he had a chance to utter a further word she yanked open the door and ran through it.

It banged against the wall before bouncing back in its frame leaving the room eerily silent. Numbed, Erik sank to the chair by the hearth. He rested his head in his hands, trying to press away the image of Anna murdering for a scrap of respect and honor.

She has lived with her own form of madness. Why can life not remain as it is here, basic in contrast to our pasts? His fingers pulsed against his mask like a spider sucking on a meal. An unwelcomed thought crept into his mind and spread like that spider's web. *What is life like at Chagny? What has the comte built being the hunter and not the hunted?*

A log hissed, and then popped. Erik rolled his head toward it. *I finally embrace the normalcy of life Philippe de Chagny so wanted for me—but at what cost? Meddling man!* Regret seeped into his soul. He deeply missed his music and knew he owed far too much of what he had to his old friend. *The time has come to merge past with the present. How does one conduct such an opera alone?*

Erik stood. He slipped out the door and found her in the kitchen courtyard. The herbs took her abuse as she snapped leaves and branches and slammed them into an awaiting basket. Approaching from behind, he reached over and put a hand on the back of her neck.

"*Mon Die—!*"

Her fist landed like a shot against his jaw as soon as she rounded. Years of torment drove forward an uncontrolled fury. Anna scratched and punched, making violent contact with whatever part of him she could.

"Anna!" Erik reached for her flailing hands. She avoided him. He reached again. Grabbing her tight to his body, he hauled her as she kicked and screamed back against the monastery wall. "Anna, hush. Anna! Anna...!" Erik lowered them to the ground, cooing softly in her ear as she writhed in his arms like a child trapped before her lifelong monster. "Anna, shhh..."

Cradling her close to his chest he held her tightly against his own racing heart in total understanding of her long overdue release. She broke down sobbing and trembling like a frightened bird. His long, thin fingers entwined with hers and he turned her small hands over in his.

"These hands did what they had to do. Mine did what I wanted. There is a difference."

Anna pressed her head back against his chest and wailed. "I want a normal life! I want my children to understand our pasts, but in the same beat of my heart I don't want them to know. They're only *children*. I never was a child, Erik. I don't want to ruin their innocence."

"I had no childhood either." He rested his mask against her hair. "I am living through them, and believe me I do not want it to end. But at some point they have to know."

"What if that was Loup? What if Simone really did hear him? What if we have to leave again? What if the children don't understand?"

There were so many questions with so few answers, and her questions merely tests he could not master. "If and when the time comes we will deal with it together, and we will tell them, slowly." Reaching around her, he dried her tears. "Thank you, *mon* Anna."

She shifted in his lap to look up at him. "For what? Lying for years? Beating you?"

"For having me tell them that I am a Maestro." His voice filled with enormous passion. "Anna, I have had so much music locked inside of me since we settled here. I feel I can share that now."

He shifted her in his lap and stroked her hair before tasting her tears. One kiss to each eye dipped them closed and drove home his love for her. Music rose in his mind, undulating up and down, repeating each note with the beat of his heart. He trailed his lips down her cheek to her nose, all along softly telling her to relax. The music leveled out before skipping through his mind, building and rising with each taste of her. Erik kept their lips as one as he stood, taking her with him.

The music that flooded his mind every time he loved her grew louder and louder until it was unbearable...unspeakable.

His eyes snapped open. He tore his kiss from hers. Shock held him firmly in place. Around them, falling from the air itself, was music unlike any ever heard. He studied Anna's face. Her eyed darted back and forth. She heard it as well.

"That is not in my mind," Erik said, ominously. "Where is it coming from?"

"I have no idea."

He traced the air with his eyes following unseen stanza's of music. It guided him around the building to behold a supernatural sight. Erik and Anna stood as still as statues, mimicking the posture of Philippe and the Brother as Simone twirled like a dervish in the courtyard.

Violin against her chin, bow to the strings she was one with the instrument and the music dancing on the air. The child skipped and spun, painting a story around her. Erik never experienced anything like it. It shifted and moved as fast as wildfire. It exploded as passionate as love itself. Dancing and bowing at the same time, her golden curls fanning around her, she didn't miss a single note. How she knew to put the notes together, he had no idea. The look on her face was a combination of raw madness and utter bliss. Erik swallowed hard. He barely heard Anna's stammered question.

"Did you ever...when you were young...how is she...?"

"I do not know. I never did...this."

Transfixed, a foreboding rose in him he dared not express. This...was unnatural. He jolted as the music jerked in a different direction, Simone's chime-like laughter adding to the notes. Her body was an extension of the music as she moved. Fear formed two hands and punched him backward. Music, when uncontrolled in his mind, lead to noise and noise led to madness.

He wouldn't have his little girl condemned.

"No!" Panic charged him forward with such ferocity Simone abruptly stopped playing. "Simone, give me the violin."

"*Nein!*" she cried with a fervor he had never heard. "These are my birds! I put them in here now! Leave them alone!"

"Simone, return my violin. Now!"

She bolted out of reach each time he swung for her. Struck dumb, the rest of his family was unable to help. Only Erik had the fierce determination to silence what he suspected was on the rise in his little girl. Finally snagging her by one arm, he hauled her firmly to his chest. She writhed like a trapped reptile as she screamed and kicked. Biting his forearm, Simone dropped to the ground taking the beloved instrument with her.

"They are *my* violin birds." She ran out of the yard as fast as her legs could carry her. "You can't have them back!"

Erik was about to make chase when Anna clamped his arm. "Let her go. She'll retreat to one of her favorite spots, calm down and all will be well. This is Simone after all."

Chest heaving, his mind racing with the poison of noise long suppressed, he turned to regard his family and the Brother Lukas. His forearm throbbed with the aftermath of a child's wrath.

"That was not Simone. That was a petite Phantom."

Chapter Five

The morning sun was dimmed by clouds, draping Paris in a monochromatic gray.

André cinched the belt on his overcoat tighter around his waist and turned the collar up to his neck. He ran his hands through his hair to tame the dampened tresses that had fallen free. He wandered up and down the rows of plants in the courtyard garden carefully selecting the flowers to enhance his bouquet.

"Picking flowers. Such a masculine past time."

André's bouquet fell to his side along with his arm. He looked around the courtyard, his jaw tightening so much he felt it in his ears. He spotted the bounty hunter leaning casually against a stone memorial.

"You really are as soft as your father," Loup continued. "You should travel with me. I'll teach you what it is like to become truly hard."

"What are you doing here?" Last night's tension wound in André anew. He hadn't enjoyed his birthday from the moment he laid eyes on Loup.

"Here, as in the garden, or here in general?" Loup indicated a prized rose bush and the English fox hound sniffing about it. "Here, I am allowing my dog to piss. In general, I am about to head out to find your Phantom."

André jerked his chin in the air. "You haven't found him in sixteen years. You are an incompetent ass."

"Rich, perhaps, but not an ass. I'm merely doing my job."

"That job, Monsieur, does not include engaging my son." André and Loup turned in tandem as Raoul approached down the center stone path. "It's a frightfully dreary day for a stroll in the garden, Vicomte." Raoul made his way up the steps to a higher level of the terraced courtyard.

41

"I was collecting a bouquet for *Maman*. She seemed upset this morning." He studied Loup. "A pity after a grand celebration."

"The only thing that will ever cheer that woman is a monster in a mask." Loup lifted his brow to Raoul and yanked on his fob. He spoke to the morning hour. "Don't tell me. Your Persian fellow denied knowing a thing about the Phantom, but you wish me to be on my merry way nonetheless."

André looked between the two significant figures in his life, his father and the creature that often roamed his nightmares. He waited on an explanation, but his father remained silent. Loup's presence in his life had long been enough to make André snap. He represented a menace as much as he did a fascinating, unattainable a part of Chagny's history.

"What's going on, Father? Loup disappears for an entire year, returns, and is now dismissed overnight? You think I don't notice how unusual that is? The Phantom is near, isn't he? He's truly been found. If such is the case, I want to know. I am the Vicomte de Chagny and I'll not have that man anywhere near my mother."

"And I'm the Comte de Chagny and head of this family. I don't bow to my son's demands."

"I wish Uncle Philippe were here."

Those words punched his father's face harder than a fist of a man five times his size. André turned his back to both of them. *I won't take them back. I refuse!*

If he had the guts he would have shoved Loup aside and off the memorial he leaned against. Though far from the elaborate crypt at Chagny, the memorial to Philippe commanded an awesome respect and Loup's boots upon its pristine surface sickened him.

"That was an abrupt confession, son. Why does Philippe's death concern you now? It never has in the past."

"How would you know? You never asked me of it in the past and Loup never disappeared for a full year only to return and cause you and Jules to whisper, and Mother to look as though she has seen a ghost. Speaking of Uncle Philippe is taboo."

Loup pushed off the memorial with a delighted laugh and swung round to snap a branch from a nearby tree. Dewy leaves shook down around them. Leaping like a deranged frog, the bounty hunter drew a line in the fine gravel path between father and son.

"Who will cross it first?" he dared. "I adore a good row between father and son! Tell me, Vicomte, what do you understand about those whispers?" Loup leaned in close to André's ear. "Who killed your dear old uncle? The same masked man who wants to bed your mother, and vice versa, or someone else?"

"What?" André's gasp colored the morning air around him a ghostly white.

"Be on your way, Monsieur!" Raoul commanded. "We have our answers from the Persian. Now get underway and do not return until you have what I want from you."

"What are those answers?" André pushed away from Loup's vile breath. "Did...did the Phantom kill Uncle Philippe?" His eyes darted from the wild glee painted on Loup's face to the rising tension coiling around his father. "I suspect something *did* happen between the Phantom and Uncle Philippe. I...I always have. Tell me now! Let me know that part of Chagny. I'm its heir, Father. Back home I see you sit in silence before his tomb and I've no answers as to why!"

"His tomb and hers." Loup returned to his previous perch and caressed the two names engraved on the memorial.

André followed his fingers with his eyes. "If you *ever* speak of my sister again I will personally run you through!" He turned to his father, more and more questions rolling in his mind. He nodded to her name. "I was told that stress the Phantom placed on Mother years ago robbed me of Evangeline and caused her still birth. Now it seems that stress makes all the more sense."

Several seconds ticked by that seemed like hours until his father's unusually calm voice broke the tension. When his father was this serious, the outcome was never good. His father indicated the half done bouquet.

"Your mother will be charmed. Bring them to her and tell her we are going for a ride. She need not know the reasons. I will tell you what I see fit and you are not to question me further."

"You give them to her." André removed a single lily and shoved the balance of the bouquet into his father's chest. "I may be getting the answers I finally deserve, but it does little to calm the anxiety of years of not knowing." Before he left, he turned to the memorial and laid the bloom beneath. "That one was for Evangeline."

His boots crunched angrily on the pebbled path, the sound beating like a drummer to the answers he was finally to receive. Halfway down the path he stopped upon hearing his father. He looked over his shoulder

"Leave, Monsieur. When you return you had best show me an end to this nightmare, for second to the Phantom there is no one I want out of my life more than you."

The bounty hunter's trademark laugh peppered the air followed by his jaunty rendition of *Alouette*. André hated that song. He kept his eyes on Loup and the dog nipping at his feet as he headed in the opposite direction. His father's back remained to him. André watched remorsefully as his father pulled a perfect red rose from the bouquet and lifted it to his nose. The rest he lay down at the base of the memorial. André's heart seized to see him press his palm over the name of Philippe Georges Marie. His father's head bowed in a palatable pain that André felt, but didn't understand.

Maybe I will soon...

Mist of a different kind threatened André's eye as he wished his uncle near. He watched his father trace the name until he could take it no more. André rushed inside. He could wish all he wanted; nothing would bring Uncle Philippe back.

* * * *

Christine indulged this hobby of his though she preferred when Raoul doted on his orchids. They at least didn't smell of hay and leather.

André's celebration seemed a distant memory in light of Loup's surprise arrival. The glamour of fine music and drink had been replaced by a stroll among the stalls. Usually such relaxed her husband, but by the way his jaw tightened making his moustache lift, he was anything but focused. Perhaps he missed his vast holdings at Chagny and it was time to return from their Paris holiday and forget the allure of the World's Fair. Or maybe his aggravation stemmed because of the ice she doused on what had been a bonding afternoon with his son. Legard walked next to him, crop taping lightly against his gloved palm. Christine stayed in place, invisible pitcher of ice water in hand.

"I merely feel as his mother I'm in within my right to know what you told him. You take Jules out for a ride to tell our family history to our son and I'm left perplexed?"

The moustache twitched again, a surefire sign his impatience was rising. He did an excellent job of hiding it in horseflesh.

"What do you wish of me, Christine? André had questions about Loup's arrival and I gave him answers."

"Only about his arrival?" She looked to Legard for answers.

"We discussed Philippe as well, in addition to my visit with the Persian."

Going to visit that Persian fellow to seek answers about Erik was a warning shot louder than cannon fire. This manhunt was about to boil out of control—again. Raoul reached into a stall, flaring a need in her to rip his hand out and slap him senseless. They were up to something, she could feel it. Petting a horse would do nothing to help calm the rising storm.

"His is old enough to know, Christine," Raoul admitted. "Including that we are inches away from finding the Phantom. What is your misgiving over this?"

"What makes you say I have any misgivings?"

"For one, your unusual silence since Loup arrived. Second, you take issue with my role as head of this family and how I elect to raise my heir." His forearm rested on a stall door. "Third, when your voice rises in pitch you're either hiding something or as nervous as a newly trained diva."

"Hiding something? Don't be ridiculous."

"See? There's that pitch again. It's time this family was involved in this manhunt on the same level. Answers to my brother's death depend on it."

Her hands slapped in exasperation to her sides. "Erik had nothing to do with Philippe's death. That is *your* private obsession. Don't allow it to color our son's perceptions."

"Don't allow it?" Raoul jolted backward. "I'll not allow it as long as your obsession is removed from the palette as well."

A lump developed in her throat. She feared the lump was visible. "What are you talking about?"

"Erik."

That name was a hot iron right to her heart.

"If we tell André everything that went on in the Garnier, about your Angel of Music and the Phantom," Raoul challenged, "then why not tell André about your obsession with *Erik* also?"

"I have no obsession, be it Angel, Phantom or man. You are the one hunting him down. This has gone on far too many years. We must move beyond it."

Lies rolled off her tongue like spun silk. If she was obsessed with anyone it Anna Barret. Erik had saved her life from a horrible man, yet her immaturity years ago fostered by jealousy toward Anna had created an avalanche of untruths.

Reaching into a stall she took her husband's cue and rubbed the soft muzzle of a mare. Her hands trembled. She perpetuated this manhunt and her conscience knew it. It could have been over years ago if she had simply told Raoul Erik saved her life. But would Raoul have believed her? Vengeance still would have seen Erik put to death. And then there was the matter of her heart... An avalanche of lies was smothering.

"I hunt him for you!" Raoul snapped. "For a promise I made to you and one I made to myself that Philippe's death wouldn't be ignored."

"You're the only one who believes Erik had anything to do with Philippe's drowning on the shores of that lake beneath the opera."

"That is unfair, Christine," Legard tried to interject.

She turned to him. "Is it? Look me in the eye and tell me, *Inspector Legard*, that you have any burden of proof. If you did, would you be scampering off to bother an old Persian every time we met with a dead end? You're André's godfather. Step in and protect him. You've become hunter worse than Loup."

"So have you," Raoul pointed out. "Do you think I don't know your reasons for reacting with such bliss every time we meet with those dead ends?"

"Bliss? You know I want nothing to do with that man. I want him captured as much as you do. I merely regret the years stolen from my family."

"Your life has been one of comfort through this all, Christine. Nothing has been stolen from us except time. And you want *everything* to do with that man. I meet dead ends with Erik and your spirits lift. You think I don't see it, but I do. We come inches from news of Anna Barret and suddenly you're a fox on the chase. We come to perhaps finding both— and you fall silent." He nodded, indicating the small skip in her step. "Even now it betrays you. Your jealousy of that woman is all supreme. It's not enough that I have given you everything I possibly can and went to hell and beyond for you. No, it's not enough for *me* to love you. You need him as well."

"Raoul," Legard softly called.

Christine yanked her head up so suddenly her hair fanned backward. She lifted a hand in the air, her palm open between her and Legard. Though she appreciated his attempt to calm the rising tone in her husband's voice, she privately admitted to needing to know his suspicions.

Raoul waved their friend aside as he ticked off reasons on his fingers. "I want to find him so he can pay his debt to society for the murders he's committed, for the injustice against Chagny and to pay for the torment he put you through. Do you think I'm so naive after all these years not to realize when I share my bed with you, in your mind's eye you're loving him?"

Silence.

Christine's hand lowered like a bird plummeting from the sky with a breast of lead shot. She stared, unseeing at the hay beneath her feet. That confrontation brewed for years. She never expected it to make her feel so dazed. Looking up, Raoul's back was turned to her as he stared intently toward the courtyard. Glancing to Legard she noted his folded arms and downtrodden stare.

"My fidelity is yours, Raoul. I gave you my life and our children."

She saw his shoulders stiffen. There was no way she could tell Raoul the feelings she had told Erik in the opera house so long ago. That she loved her husband with all her heart, but Erik with all her soul. What was more powerful, loving from the heart or the soul? How could anyone save her understand what it was like to be chosen by the Angel of Music? What it meant to love two men ardently, but differently?

She turned to a nearby mare and stared into her brown eyes. She barely saw her reflection in them. *Lord, your mercy, please. Don't let him see in my eyes he is right! Sometimes I do think of Erik in that way. I must. I love him. I long to experience the man his kiss showed to me...not an Angel, not a Phantom, but my dark, mysterious, and deeply sensual man.* She inched her head over her shoulder to look at Raoul. *I need them both, don't I? Raoul is my necessity in life, the Phantom my pure desire. Lord, how do I separate the two? I don't want to. I love them both.*

"I gave you our children," she whispered, begging her soul for control. "You've nothing to say to that?"

Raoul glanced beyond Paris to the direction of Chagny. She caught his eye when he moved. The mention of their children, not just André, lifted sadness behind them. Losing their baby due to the stress of a manhunt was just one more lie she tattooed upon her soul.

Closing her eyes she fought aside the memory of Loup shoving her while pregnant down that flight of stairs.

If only I had consented to his blackmail demands immediately! Evangeline was lost because of Loup's abuse of me and his threats upon her life. I was desperate to spare you, Raoul. Spare you the scandal my secrets would bring Chagny.

Even in that death, Raoul blamed Erik. In it all Christine blamed herself, but there was no way to climb free of her lies. She loved Erik, she had always loved him, and faced with a choice right this moment, she would choose...

André.

Oh, dear God...

Her son! She pressed a shaking hand to her mouth. What was she doing? Selfishly trying to decide which man would love her more, her husband or the Phantom, when the one who loved her the most was barely a man.

Christine felt her cheeks drain of color. Coming up behind her husband, she wrapped her arms around his waist. "I chose you, Raoul. From the beginning I chose you, and now you and

André." She nodded at Legard silently asking for his forgiveness as well. "Deal with the Persian, tell our son what you will, do what you may with Loup. Find Erik."

Don't find, Erik! I don't know what to do, but I pray you will never will find him...so help me, I pray you never will!

She reached up and brushed her lips softly to his. She secretly forced her soul to obey her, lying to the voices in the mind in order to do battle with her own demons; the longing she so desperately had for a man she shouldn't love.

Chapter Six

Anna compared the sun and the position of the tree's shadow. She had been waiting nearly thirty minutes. With no roof overhead, the late afternoon sun beat upon her shoulders and made the granite flecks in the stones around her glimmer to life. Squinting did little to lessen the glare. What had been the church stood in throbbing silence despite the chattering birds. Waiting patiently, she watched Erik move among the rubble. He was an ardent disbeliever in God. He didn't come here to mourn what the building represented. With his face perpetually caged, Anna had come to learn the small twitches of his hands or slight tilts to his head that betrayed his moods. When he came to the steps that had once led to the organ, his mood worsened.

"You're contemplating telling him everything, aren't you, beyond your history as a reclusive Maestro? That's why you're roaming among rubble."

The subject had been capped weeks ago, leaving her to deal with the fissure created between father and son. He and Philippe were often at odds. They were two genius minds constantly working to trump one another. Since learning his father was a Maestro, something shifted in Philippe. The boy long adored music. Soaking up all he could at village fairs, often spending time with the monks as they played Erik's organ. His father refused to touch the instrument—even refused to speak about music—a point Philippe never understood until now. With the new revelations regarding Chagny and the manhunt, it became all too obvious just how sharp Philippe's mind truly was, leaving Anna to ponder how much longer her son wouldn't press the issue.

Erik turned to stare down the center aisle to where she stood. Anna patiently folded her hands over the basket of eggs for the market. She knew he wouldn't answer her query.

Standing there, in fading sunshine, dressed head to toe in black with his face still, unnecessarily, concealed behind a mask, a foreboding God-like quality poured out of his stance. It sent a ripple down her spine. She had a thrilling respect for Erik's power and passion, and a melancholy realization for how he came to be that way. He was a living oxymoron. Fitting into this sort of world—but not. She lifted her chin higher in surprise when he spoke.

"Philippe, I could use your help with what is left of the organ."

Philippe stood at what had been the door, refusing to enter the charred remains of the building. In the street beyond, the village vibrated with its usual pace. Carriages rumbled down the road and townsfolk hustled about. The realization of his father's odd history at the Garnier clearly was a mantel on his youthful shoulders more so then the sack of wool slung over them. Philippe didn't move beyond shifting his weight to his opposite leg. He was impatient. Anna repressed a need to sigh and glanced from son to father.

"Does that reply answer your question?" Erik frowned.

The twittering of a violin met their ears. Their daughter, however, was positively vibrant. The violin hadn't ceased its music since she found it. Her current tune mirrored her nimble mischief—warbling notes up and down like the call of a far-off blackbird. She walked in circles near her brother as she played, never once paying any regard to the chatter of familiar villagers as they paused to listen before continuing on their way. She preferred music of late, allowing notes to fall out of her fingers instead of words out her mouth.

Anna flicked her eyes from Simone to Erik. His shoulders hadn't relaxed since Simone found her music, and seeing her march around Philippe only stiffened him more. It did nothing of the sort for Anna. The ease in which Simone played was a mysterious blessing. In light of the idea that Chagny had been lurking weeks ago, and now with Philippe's silence, Anna looked to find anything that was a simple joy. To Erik her music seemed a potential curse.

"Simone!"

Philippe's cry snapped Anna out of her introspection. Her heart slamming against her ribs as she spun toward him, eggs flew out of the basket, splattering around her feet. Erik raced past her in a blur of black. Anna followed as fast as her legs could carry her.

Simone cowered at her brother's feet, wide-eyed, dazed, with one tiny hand coated with the blood from her temple. Philippe's head volleyed around him.

"She was playing and out of nowhere—a rock!"

The stone at her foot was equally coated red.

"Simone?" Erik sank to his knees.

"Somebody knocked my birds quiet and made the notes mean," she said hollowly.

Anna knew that look on her face. She had seen it hundreds of times before in her life, always when a situation arose that Simone didn't understand. Erik's expression she didn't need to see. A pole seemed to replace his spine.

"I'm sure a carriage simply kicked up a rock." She reached out to undo the kerchief at her daughter's neck. "All will be well."

Philippe stood, his face twisting into an angry scowl. "No one is going to hurt her and get away with it." His hands balled into fists as he searched around him. He started toward a crowd at the green, but Erik's hand shot out. It encircled his wrist.

"Philippe, no," he sternly said.

"No? People can't just—"

"People are a despicable lot. They can, and they will."

Erik's tone was gentle enough as he studied Simone's wound, but its undercurrent coursed with repressed outrage.

"I'm certain it was just a carriage," Anna insisted. A seven year old's world is only so big and the thought of prejudice making her daughter's world smaller was a fear she'd been battling since Simone's birth. They refused to see her masked merely to spare man their misgivings about those who looked different.

"How can you be so caviler?" Philippe was incredulous. "People can, granted, but they won't because I'll not have it!"

Anna held her hand up insisting her son remain calm. She patted his arm, acknowledging the dismay that pinched his eyes. "Philippe, enough." Simone rolled the rock around in her hands, her long hair scattering around her lap like a security blanket.

"Look at her, Father. She doesn't understand these things!"

Anna bit her tongue. Philippe was Simone's exclusive champion and at times like this his passion to protect all consuming.

Erik carefully lifted bloody hair out of her wound strand by matted strand. "Simone understands in ways she knows how." Erik's eyes met Anna's, making her frown. "I always did."

"It was a carriage." Anna stood, kerchief in hand. Placing a kiss on her daughter's head she nodded toward the distant creek snaking the outskirts of the village center. "I'll soak this in water. A carriage is to blame, nothing more."

Heading off, she rubbed her temple. A massive headache was on the prowl. Looking behind her to where Simone sat, Erik tending her and Philippe standing sentry, she sighed heavily.

I wish I could crawl into that child's head and understand how she puzzles through the world. The music she would play after this would shift, perhaps a long and sad piece. The tunes seemed to match the look on her face, and all Anna saw in her haunted eyes now was the same distant regard for the world present in Erik's.

She knelt at the water's edge and soaked the kerchief. The light shimmered off the water.

It was no carriage. As much as I want to believe it, I know it was not. Our sleepy village teems with hunters gearing up for stag season now. It is only a matter of time before she tastes the world that lay beyond this village. A taste of how some people embrace her with compassion while others will embrace her with fear. She angrily twisted the kerchief. *Come what may, I will not see her masked. I will not!*

Glancing over her shoulder, her heart shattered a thousand times as Simone curled her hand over her face and placed the red stone in her pocket. It would be a scar she would keep forever. Even from a distance Anna could see the agony pouring off Erik for her confusion and pain.

Wringing out the kerchief, the water distorted the quivering reflections in the creek. The natural mirror in front of her reflected a warped face. She cocked her head and leaned down to study the reflection.

What is that? Who—

Anna gasped. Her chest seized. The blood in her heart dripped dry and pooled at her feet. Her eyes lifted from the wet, black boots to the man looming over her.

"*Mon alouette*. It has been awhile hasn't it?"

Water smacked her in the face as the man slammed a fist of rocks down into the creek. Bile shot to her throat. "Loup..."

"Oh, *mon aloutte*, say it again." A lewd moan snaked out his mouth seconds before he lunged.

His hand smelled of filth as he clamped it over her mouth. Tree branches whipped her face and tore at her ankles as she was dragged away. They stopped short.

"I knew you were here when I burned down that church." Loup's teeth slammed against hers as he ravaged her mouth with his unforgiving greeting. He broke the kiss and seconds later whispered hotly in her ear. "Your old friend the comte wants proof you and your lover are here. He will get more than proof, won't he?" Loup nodded back toward the green. "I suspect your Phantom will be absolutely raging when he finds you missing. He will come running after you, doing my job for me—making a dull manhunt pure delight. I get to sit back and enjoy the show. Life is beautiful."

Anna's heart threatened to pound out of her chest as she was hauled to a clearing. She fought, but he held her so tightly it was all she could do to breathe. As soon as he gave her some slack to undo the tether on his horse she thought to run, but the hounds surrounding her began growling at her scent.

If she had one phobia, it was dogs.

"Tell me, *mon aloutte*, did you miss me?" Loup snatched her by the waist and slammed her back against the trunk of a tree. Tears sprung to her eyes. He hitched her upon his hips forcing her legs about his waist and ground his need hard against her. Anna bit her cheek until she tasted blood, and refused to look at the dogs inching closer. Loup nipped a path up her neck stilling her ability to scream.

"You've been busy I see. You've children." He rocked against her. "Your daughter is positively horrific. I hope that rock didn't hurt her. I couldn't resist a bit of target practice."

He circled inside her ear with this tongue. "Why so quiet, *Alouette*? You are shocked to see me? The hunt for you has kept me delightfully engaged over all these years, but nothing is quite as sweet as holding your trophy buck. Surely you knew my services were employed by the comte? He will be pleased, as will others who are dying to see you." He stressed his words, his smile leaching a perverse satisfaction. "Mainly a certain Belgian duke."

"I don't know what you're talking about," she whispered shakily.

"I figured you would say that. But no fears, you'll soon find out."

Anna's cry was stifled by the crushing force of his lips against hers. The kiss was harsh and violent, squeezing moisture out her eyes. Thrashing her head side to side, she shook him off.

"So sweet a reunion." Loup laughed.

Her world pitched as he swung her on to the horse. Dogs leapt and snapped at her feet. Body rigid with fear, she was powerless to stop the inevitable as he mounted behind her and spurred the horse into action.

Erik's name tore from her soul seconds before the horse bolted forward.

* * * *

Simone's eyes were closed. She perched upon the railing of a fence near the village center, her head moving gracefully back and forth in time with the sad, yet perplexing tune weeping out of her violin. Erik folded his arms across his chest, attempting to keep his eyes from the bright red mark upon her temple. Philippe leaned against the fence, studying each villager that passed as if they were all suspect. Several they knew stopped to listen and comment on Simone's unheard of new gift. Erik treated them with more benefit of the doubt than his son. Hearing his name, he turned as the portly owner of the post wobbled in his direction. He paused to listen to the mournful notes for a moment before handing Erik a letter and hastening off.

Beneath his mask, Erik's face skewed as much as Simone's music shifted. Livelier notes skipped on the air as she hopped off the fence to play merrily to the flock of chickens pecking their way across the green. Hearing her thoughts shift away from the cut on her head lifted his heart from his stomach back to its rightful place. His nerves, however, stood at the ready.

He glanced at the note with circumspect caution. It was addressed to him care of the abbot. Suspicion descended and he looked at it through shuttered eyes. Wrinkled and stained, it clearly had undergone quite a journey to find him. He unfolded it.

Know one thing if this does reach you. I want nothing to do with you, yet the rumination of our past cannot be ignored. Last we met I recall a babe in your arms. I do this only for his sake. Chagny has found you. Wherever you are, leave—Vahid.

Erik lifted his eyes from the note to Philippe and Simone's concerto for chickens. For the second time in a span of minutes his name rent the air. This time it was personal.

"Anna?"

Philippe shoved off the fence. "Father, she sounded—"

Erik cut him off with one sharp slice of his hand. He knew what it sounded like—and it didn't sound pleasant. He lifted Simone from her rapt feathered audience and called Anna's name as he headed across the green toward the creek. He called her name again to no avail.

"Father?" Philippe pointed to the ground as they approached and to the wet, dust-covered kerchief. "Whose boot prints are those?"

Erik's blood pumped harder counting the two sets of prints. "Go to Brother Lukas. Give him this." He thrust the note into his son's hand. "Tell him to pack my satchel, ready the horse, and do not set foot from the monastery."

"Why?" Philippe shook open the letter and read hastily. "What's going on? Who is Vahid? Where's Mother?"

Erik shoved Simone into Philippe's arms as he allowed his fury to billow. "Go now."

"Father, what—"

"Now!"

Philippe's curse and Simone's sudden tears went unnoticed as his children raced away. Erik's focus was on the tree line and the perverse fury pumping through his body. If hatred were flames, the entire forest would be ablaze.

"*Anna!*" No response. Turning, he tried to grasp the direction they went. "*Anna!*"

He pushed through the thick brush. It would be so easy to give into the madness boiling the surface of his brain, allowing that part of him to take full control of the situation. But what of the promise he made years ago to Philippe de Chagny not to prostitute his anger ever again? A small tree bent and snapped. Erik growled and thrust it aside.

"Anna!"

Past promises could go to hell. No one would destroy what he had gained. Branches ripped as he tore a path through the woods. No one would rob him of Anna. Erik paused once in the clearing. A deadly silence surrounded him save for the noise in his head. Noise he hadn't heard in a very long time.

There was only one place he could go from here. Only one place where he had allies.

The Opera Garnier.

A haunting voice drifted from him as the Phantom unwillingly clawed its way out of his soul.

"Raoul de Chagny, be careful what you steal from me..."

Chapter Seven

Weeks being dragged like Loup's dog on a leash to end up in Paris were all too surreal. The early dawn light shown through the high window casting Anna's shadow across an intricate marble floor. She stared at it as it fell across the small patterns and saw nothing other than the strange silhouette around her face. Watching her shadowy hand as it explored her naked neck, she was too numb to experience any emotion. Without the weight of her braid snaking against her back her entire body felt foreign. Loup's resounding laughter still vibrated in her ears when, halfway to Paris, his knife had sliced it clear off her neck cropping her waist-long hair to her chin. Preparation for her life in prison he triumphantly announced, when she knew better.

It was a trophy and this is no prison that's for sure. I would have preferred a stone cold cell to Loup bringing me to the mouth of this lion.

The salon she was in reeked of Chagny. She slept little on the tedious journey out of Germany and smiled sadly to the doors where outside two footmen stood guard.

Without doubt, I bet the comte is having a rude awakening to my arrival.

Exhaustion enveloped her. Every muscle ached and she tongued the inside of her jaw, prodding her bruised cheek. She calmed her racing heart and aching body by thinking of her children.

Where are they? What pieces of the puzzle are falling into place for them? They will understand soon enough, knowing Erik. What mother does this to her children?

She followed a trail of dust traitorously highlighted by the sun up toward the window. Erik would descend upon Paris soon. The sense of him wound around her core and pulled her like nothing else could. Once Erik found her missing, he would begin at the past and the past reared an ugly head.

I have to get to the Garnier!

The doorknob clicked. The doors flung open. Anna jumped. Loup bobbed his way into the room like a maniacal pied piper.

"*Bon Matin, mon alouette!*" He stopped inches before her and glanced to a small silver tray. "Why, you've not touched your food. The fine fare not to your liking? Perhaps you were expecting a pint of gruel and molasses, a bit of bread and some salt?" Loup flung himself into a massive wing chair. "I thought it would be more fun to toy with you here than a prison. The shock on the comte's face was positively delightful when I informed him of this little stunt. Having you here allows me to watch your pretty little face writhe in dismay at what may come next."

"I am hardly dismayed."

Did fear or anger flare her nostrils? Loup's hand shot out. He snatched her wrist and pulled her to him. Anna muffled a cry as her knees slammed against the floor. The momentum pitched her forehead forward, burying her face against Loup's obvious arousal. She instantly yanked her head of his lap.

His hand grabbed the sides of her jaw forcing her to remain in her submissive position. The flesh beneath his thumb and forefinger began to burn under his grip. Anna winced. He tilted her face up slightly so their eyes could meet. His gleaming wolf-like teeth, contrasted the rotting stench that accented each word.

"Make my life easy while we are here, *Alouette*, and tell the comte what he wants to know. The sooner you do, the sooner you and I can be on to more delectable pursuits toward Belgium." She writhed. He smiled. "Unless you are anxious to begin now?" Loup's opposite hand reached for the buttons on his trousers.

Anna spat in his face.

"You whore!" He tossed her aside, laughing as she hit the floor in front of him. He used his shirt sleeve to swipe his face. "No time anyway, *Alouette*." A curt nod directed her attention to the sounds in the hall. She scrambled to all fours, then her feet. "Seems like you are about to meet some old friends."

A bonfire ignited in her belly as soon as Legard and the Comte de Chagny entered. Anna bit her tongue. Years later and still the sight of them could fold her skin inside out. A bitter taste flooded her mouth and she fought the urge to twirl and spit it at their feet. Years upon years of injustice for a crime committed in self-defense! The air in the small room, already unbearably stuffy, thickened.

"As soon as she tells me what I need, you may contact the Belgian authorities," the comte said to Legard.

Anna's last meal threatened to reappear on her shoes. Not that it would be much. Loup wasn't exactly gracious in his care for her.

"Mademoiselle Barret, we meet again."

She ignored him.

"It barely seems possible," Raoul said incredulously. "Not even a month ago I was enjoying the opera and fair wondering if this moment would ever come. You've nothing to say?"

Anna stiffened as Loup's hand slapped on top of her head and twisted her around. Using the momentum, she stumbled to the side and out of his way. Raoul's eyes flared wide before they shot to the bounty hunter to her right making a satisfied huff jump out her mouth.

Let him look horrified. The bruises fading from purple to sickly yellow on her face would turn any stomach. *He should see the bruising Loup left on my thighs.*

"Monsieur le Comte." Her voice was monotone.

Raoul tugged the immaculate sleeves of his waistcoat and strode further into the room. "I don't see the point in wasting words, Mademoiselle, since you will be off to a trial shortly. Where is he?"

"Trial for *what*, Monsieur?"

"Kidnapping, robbery, murder, aiding, abetting, arson ..." The comte spread his hands as his brows shot up. "Do you have any idea what it cost me to rebuild the carriage house?"

Anna shrugged. "You forget. I stole your horse as well—a worthy and hefty crime."

He tried to contain his impatience, she could tell by his shifting expressions, but it leached out in the hole he attempted to wear in the floor. "Don't try my patience. Where is he?"

"Where is who?"

"I figured you would be difficult. The Phantom. I suspect you have been with him."

"I know no Phantoms, Monsieur."

"Fine then. *Erik*."

"I've been alone for many years." Her speech was well rehearsed, not that he could tell. "I was quite surprised you wanted me so badly." She looked at Loup. "But you obviously have your reasons."

"So you've no idea where he is?"

Anna tried hard not to roll her eyes as she continued to spoon feed him her story. "We became separated a few months after the fire. I haven't seen him since. I continued on alone."

"Was he to follow you?"

"I had no association with him after that. Perhaps Erik is with the diva. That is the way the story should be written, isn't it?"

The comte looked annoyed.

"Mademoiselle, I suggest you find the answers I need quickly. Your life will be in prison after this. Enjoy your comfort while you can. It will only be a matter of time before I transport you to Belgium."

She kept her eyes upon him until they all left the room. She only slammed them shut when Loup blew her a kiss that sent ice down her spine. The door latched behind them, locking her in the most bizarre prison she ever inhabited. Though the door muffled the sound, she heard Raoul's voice clear enough.

"Alert the authorities and the theater police. Doubtful Erik is around as he has yet to be in any opera house anywhere, and he'd be a fool to show up here, but I am not taking chances. I want all of Paris on this." As she heard their footsteps start to move away, she caught the first strands of a weariness color his voice. "Fetch my physician to tend to her jaw."

* * * *

The past became a shadow, trailing him across the countryside of Germany and France. Throughout it all he wasn't at peace, barely keeping his madness repressed. The first time they left a horse behind at a train station threatened to crack Erik in two. The memories came upon in wave after wave. Each boxcar they stowed away on churned things he elected never to remember. It flamed his anger toward Chagny.

Somber and silent, Philippe barely spoke as they criss-crossed their way back to Paris. The only topic he was willing to discuss was music, an element missing from the last time he spent life on the run. He would speak of it and his only other obsession—his sister. Hopping trains and sleeping in vagabond camps had turned her music into a hodgepodge of emotions. It kept a sour taste in Erik's mouth. All she knew was that village and the normal life it gave her. This life and world she didn't understand. It made him guilty that this pursuit had cracked its way into her mind, questioning her innocent outlook on the world.

Distant lights glowed in the night far ahead. Paris lay before them and what more could he do but study the lights with bitter regret of the past. If the past kept following him—he no longer liked what Paris represented because of what it did to his kin. He watched the lights pulse in his vision, remembering his self-inflicted prison deep below ground where little of Paris reached. Only one thought kept him from wallowing in a pit of resentment. Few ever ventured to the bowels beneath the Garnier—few but Anna. She would be his saving grace.

He needed her.

Philippe's voice jolted him from his thoughts.

"Do you want me to take her, Father?"

The night was a crisp and star-filled. Erik scanned them, his mind filling with all sorts of noise, music, and memories. Philippe laid a hand on his shoulder and stroked the blanket of curls as Simone slept in his arms.

"No, let her sleep."

Erik didn't care about carrying her extra weight; she was light compared to the burdens he had bared in the past and compared to whatever demons he'd created for her. They walked for awhile, Philippe just as silent as he in the scrutiny of the stars. A second question from Philippe broke his thoughts.

"There is still more I want to know. A Maestro is one thing, The Phantom of the Opera entirely another. Since we are heading to the belly of the beast, don't you think I should know everything? Why do you perpetually avoid my questions of how you came to—"

"Be content to dwell on what I allow you to know." A fog was growing in Erik's mind and it was choking out his ability to think. "Focus on the music. It will do you well. For some, music only births madness."

"Music speaks what words cannot in my opinion. It has nothing to do with madness or if a man is mad or not."

"It all depends on what you hear *behind* the notes. You do not wish to know all that lies in my mind."

"*All* as in the stigma of the Phantom being a madman? You are no madder than Simone is truly daft."

Erik's arms curled tighter around his daughter, thankful she couldn't hear such words in her sleep. "Simply repress her music and cage these—birds—of hers while we are here and ask no more questions of me."

"Father, if the de Chagny estate is looking for us—"

"Chagny!" Erik's voice boomed like thunder, making Philippe suddenly flinch. He lowered it for Simone's sake. "Every last one of them can rot in hell. I will not have the life I finally command be a prisoner to the Chagny name. I will not, I tell you! Erik will not!"

"*Erik* will not? Since when do you refer to yourself like *that?*"

Erik gnashed his teeth and wrestled down the noise rising behind the music. Philippe stared at him with a crimped face. "I gave them everything. Their lives, liberty, and love, and damn this all that I cannot have the same in return."

"Damn this all?" Philippe stopped short. Dust and pebbles scattered around him. "Damn *you*, Father!" He hardened his stance. "My mother is abducted, my sister forced into a life she will *never* understand, and you refuse to tell me *every last thing I need to know to help*—"

"You should not have to help! You should not have found out about us in such abrupt means. Mark my words, I will not allow my family to bear the scars of Chagny's obsession with me; it is bad enough that Simone already does." He slid aside her hair to reveal the fresh scar on her temple.

Erik spun away, his angry strides putting distance between them in a matter of seconds. Clinging to Simone with every ounce of passion he had, his pain that night could have dimmed all the stars in heaven.

* * * *

His timing was off...

Morning isn't when he had wanted to arrive on the city outskirts. Erik had taken to traveling mostly in the cover of darkness, making a camp long enough for his daughter to fall asleep before taking to the road again. Moving with caution though the alleyways and channels of a city just waking was far easier when he was a Phantom. Doing so with two alert children proved a challenge. He kept his head down and hood up taking care to conceal his mask. No chances were taken. With his legacy pounded into Paris tighter then the cobbles under his feet, Erik doubted such a city would have forgotten him after so many years. Philippe and Simone flanked him, a compete juxtaposition from the last time he wove his way through the back alleys of the city, angry, shot, and on the run.

"Is this really Paris?" Wonder filled Philippe's voice.

Erik yanked him by his collar back into a shadow for a fifth time. This was Paris—but not the Paris he remembered. The extraordinary took over his city and a carnavalesque atmosphere hummed around him like mad bees in a hive. People swarmed everywhere. Fantastic displays, an inventor's dream, lined the streets at every turn. Performers roamed with outstretched hands like hungry minstrels searching for fresh ears. Great new buildings rose as if coming from Atlantis itself and the entire world seemed to lie at Paris's feet. Rising far in the distance was an abomination Erik had never seen, a massive tower that jutted from the streets to the heavens. Curiosity bellowed at him to explore the transformation of his beloved realm. With so many roaming about lost in the bustle of it all, Erik would hardly be noticed, but he refused to take a chance. A massive poster haphazardly splayed on the side of a coach advertised the traveler's destination: The World's Fair...

Philippe spun with almost every step he took. Any anger he harbored had, for the moment, been caged beneath a mask of wonderment. The aromas of sidewalk cafés and bakeries, the sounds of hooves on cobbles were all foreign to his children, as was the din of Parisians as they hustled to and fro. Awe-worthy buildings, magnificent structures, and fantastic places greeted

Philippe at every corner and out of the three, he was the only one capable of blending in outside the fairgrounds. If he could, Erik would have fostered this delight in him, but he had more pressing things on his mind.

Mainly, attempting to breathe...

Simone clung to his neck as tightly as she could, seemingly in utter horror of the sights. Trying to shift her, Erik lifted the hood of her cloak over her face. Her one hand not grasping the violin and bow was clamped tightly over her normal ear. She whimpered over the sounds complaining they chattered louder than her birds.

"Who will help us find Mother in all this?" Philippe's query was an invisible slap across Erik's face.

One problem vexed that solution. He knew it in advance but it still sat awkwardly on his shoulders. Misfortune met with Madame Giry, the old box keeper, years ago ending in her demise. She was his one true servant in life and now, gone. Had circumstances been different he would have kept in contact with her more through the years, and her death gave Erik a sword thrust of pain. The news was discovered some years ago as he wove his way across France, avoiding Chagny at every turn. The loss of her servitude had made the manhunt even more unbearable. Knowing she would always be an ally was a salve to what he put Anna and his children through.

What to do with them now? He couldn't have them wait in the Garnier while he avenged Anna's kidnapping.

There was a part of Erik that was a natural survivor and he focused on that instead of his son's impassioned questions. Fate returned him to this place, but it did not have to return his children. With Madame Giry watching him from the heavens there was only one other place he could go.

Hell wasn't an option.

* * * *

"Whatever you do, do not move from this stoop." Erik looked up and down the road satisfied they were safely tucked out of sight. "Wait here until a man either comes out of that door, or enters it. He will have jade eyes and an annoying sense of fashion."

Erik had no idea of the Persian's current habits. Not like in the past when he was as a boil festering in his life—always

65

there and just barely about to burst. This was the last place he wished to deposit his children, but it was better than doing as Philippe had said and bringing them to the belly of the beast. Until he had a chance to calm the rising noise in his mind, Philippe and Simone were better off far away from the Garnier, and Erik best off far away from the Daroga of Mazendaran.

Without Anna's guidance he wasn't half the man he could be.

"Stay here?" Philippe gasped. "I am not staying on some corner like a street rat, Father. We are going with you."

"Do as I say!"

"Do as you say when I have no idea what I'm to do?"

"What you are to do is to keep your sister safe. Keep her hood up, her face away from everyone. Do not allow her to play that violin, do you hear me? Not one note. This place will only do her harm and I cannot, I will not...Philippe!" Erik grabbed his son's shoulders and shook him sternly. The noise in his mind was like shards of glass wiggling their way through his skull. "Please," he pleaded. "Keep her away. Away from me. Away from the opera house...simply away until I—"

"Until you *what*?"

One glance from the persecution behind Philippe's crystal blue eyes to Simone's golden ones was all Erik needed to set him over the edge. The choice was simple. Stay and wrestle his rising demons in front of them, or retreat until sane enough to think clearly? Grabbing his son's cheeks in both his hands he searched his eyes, ignoring the way the boy squirmed and scowled. If Philippe continued to challenge him, he would crumble like rubble and spare not a detail to his brilliant heart. Was it worth the risk to lose his son's love forever?

Erik released Philippe's face as if on fire, and vanished into the Paris streets. The World's Fair would have no idea who it swallowed. The voice of a master ventriloquist swirled around his children as he disappeared into shadow.

"*Vous savez je t'aime...*"

It was all Erik could do to hope his children knew he loved them.

Chapter Eight

Erik retraced steps that years ago he wore like a second skin. Paris had once been his to command when he permitted himself the luxury of leaving his tomb. Shadows cloaked him all his life, so melting into them and flowing through the streets was second nature. The blessing of the bizarre surroundings of a fair in full sail added to his cloak of stealth. People and police were preoccupied; all of Paris had its focus elsewhere. His was narrowed like a hunter in quest of his meal. His search of the magistrate and the prisons turned up empty. Even as a wanted man, he arrogantly prostituted his talents enough upon unsuspecting street urchins willing to find him information for a bit of coin. Though he should be grateful Anna wasn't locked in some dank cell, he was not. Erik fought a twisting disconnect from the world around him. It billowed like ash from a volcano within him with each stone he unturned only to find Anna not there.

He scurried like a rat away from his children and shunned the light of day until the familiar catacombs seeped their dampness back into his bones. The pain the darkness created was old and familiar, but did little to calm his perverse anger. The only rays of light he clung to were those last words he spoke to his children. The bottomless black reaches far below the Opera Garnier which had once provided him with peace and respite, still had the power of birthing a cavernous hole in his heart. Nothing made him feel hollowed then losing his Anna and leaving his children behind to wonder who, or what, their father had become.

What Erik became, was angry...

Eerily, as if waking from a still dream, he looked around to see everything as he left it. Arriving on the banks of the underground lake, the boat still stood where he last moored it. If he closed his eyes he could recall Christine stepping from it as vividly as he could recall Raoul's bullet tearing through his arm. Erik swore if he looked down, scarlet would be coating his sleeve.

The boat hadn't held up over the years, but served its purpose without sinking. After a silent row across inky blackness that should have saved his senses, he docked at the entrance to his drawing room. The single candle he swiped from an office above was his only light until he got more candelabras lit. Such wasn't easy. Old wax doesn't burn well.

He had forgotten how quiet it was, oddly beautiful too. As the light grew and his eyes adjusted to the soft glow, Erik surveyed his domain. It held up to a degree over the years, surprisingly surging relief through his veins. Everything was still damp and cold, and rats found their way into his scores. Somewhere in this labyrinth was a very musical nest.

Dangerous notes tripped through his mind. He crept toward the organ lining the wall to his chambers as if it were the forbidden fruit. Reaching out Erik touched the cold metal pipes. Rust coated his hand. He continued on in his inspection stepping gingerly over the remnants of a past rage, to the room beyond, lighting candles he passed.

The memories of his last moments down there swirled like the mist on his lake. He remembered cradling Christine in his arms as he lay her down in the Louis-Philippe room, recalling how nervously he waited for her to wake, and in the confrontation that followed, how drastically his life had changed.

Erik stared intently at the coffin standing in the center of the room on a small platform. The sight of it coiled around him as he fought the head-on collision of his past and the present. He closed his eyes to the memory of sleeping in that, choosing instead to evoke the various makeshift beds he shared through the years with his Anna: hay one night, a bedroll the next. If lucky and not in an area known, perhaps warm linens in a local tavern. Tuning everything out, he listened. The only sound he heard was the distant yet comforting lap of water against the shore outside as it wrestled for a spot next to the building noise in his mind. In essence it was the heartbeat of his womb. Opening his eyes, they roamed over the red brocade fabric hanging over the coffin to read the stave of the Dies Ires on the wall. Several stories above him was the opera house, living in silent oblivion to his return and a city unprepared to meet the rage exploding within him. One second longer without Anna—the pacifier of his madness—and Paris would reverberate with a Phantom they had never met. The theater was clueless to the thoughts in his head, ignorant to the woman he missed, and unaware of the titled man he sought to kill.

Kill.

That single word jolted him as if lightning struck from the blue. Erik's face contorted beneath his mask. Body twisting into the memories, he fought the image of Philippe Georges Marie, Comte de Chagny from his mind. Fought to shove aside the memories of his only friend and the life he insisted he lead beyond that of a Phantom. But like ghosts, those memories floated around him, passing through things on their way to penetrate another. Everywhere he looked he remembered Philippe.

With noise tangoing with the music in his mind, he left his chambers and absently studied his house with new eyes. How had he ever lived down here? No sunlight, no children laughing, no one sharing his bed. He caught sight of himself in one of the still shiny pipes of his organ and chanced looking out of the corner of his eye. Mirrors, no matter the sort, were implements of pain and none existed in his life since Anna. The only reflection he needed to see of himself was the one in her eyes. He looked anyway at the rounded and distorted figure.

His mask was seamless with the ebony of his dress and blended beautifully with his clothing. Though looking nothing like the Maestro of his past, his finer clothing shed long ago for a life on the run, he still portrayed an odd elegance. He took a good, hard look at that reflection, unable to tear his eyes away. He arrived a carpenter, desired to be a Maestro and still reflected a Phantom.

With a shout that echoed vehemently across his home, Erik's arm cut across his body, clearing the contents of a nearby table. Old inkbottles, blotters, nibs and paper scattered through the air. Grasping its sides until his pallid knuckles went whiter, he stared at himself. The reflection mocked him; it wanted something of him. Memories, once reopened, can sting if allowed. An urge to unmask time and expose it for the cruel judge it was rose in him to the point he could no longer govern man versus madman. He suddenly felt the need to distance himself from the labyrinth. He had to, lest he unleash those maddening notes on Paris and Anna be made to suffer. He needed to be near those who did not know a Phantom.

He needed his children.

Erik never left that house on the lake so quickly.

* * * *

The dark fur on his Astrakhan hat turned white against the onslaught of snow. The wintry visitor was shockingly early for this time of year and highly annoying. Head bent against the weather, he cussed the disgusting slurry coating his boots and soaking the hem of his trousers. A simple trip to satisfy a craving at the local patisserie had turned into an affair that took hours. He lingered far too long attempting to avoid the weather, the only good coming of it being the second helping of a poppy seed tart. Like any other caught in this mess, he simply wanted to arrive home, pour something strong and settle down in the warmth to regard the snow in a more comfortable light.

The streets were crowded with businessmen and young lovers hastening to shelter, or fair-goers craving more excitement, making Vahid dodge and weave his way toward his flat. The closer he got to his home the streets began to clear. Such was unusual near the Tuileries, for the gardens drew crowds no matter the weather. Curious, he slowed his steps. Braving the snow stinging his eyes, he stopped, scowling at a distant crowd gathered in the vicinity of his building's door.

Instinct kicked up an uneasy feeling in his gut. Spending years as the chief of police to Persia's Sultana, he had a wariness for crowds. They usually didn't bode well, especially not on a snowy Paris morning. Nothing he could think of would make any traveler stop in their efforts to get home.

Until he heard the music...

A low mournful tune force his feet forward. The lone strands of a violin wept through the air matching the muffled mood of the snow. The closer he got the more mesmerized he became by the melody. Heads in the back of the crowed craned to catch a glimpse of the violinist as curious onlookers braved slipping on the tips of their toes to see.

Another wandering troubadour on his way to the fair perhaps?

Several in front of him swayed slowly, matching the seductive sounds. The distinct clinks of coins hitting what cobbles weren't covered in slush, occasionally poked through the weeping notes. Whispers rippled through the crowd of the child's magnificence on the strings.

Child?

The crowd was several people deep, making Vahid shoulder his way forward. When the music slowed and almost stopped, applause filled the air. As if the encouragement were a cue to change the feeling behind the piece, so changed the music. So sudden was the shift it jolted Vahid like a scorpion's sting.

Spinning, rising and skipping through the air the melody became a wild and lively jaunt through the splendor of happiness. The crowd clapped in rhythm to the tune. Awestruck chatter replaced curious whispers and soon even the downtrodden and wet were tapping their feet to match the music. Finally in a position to see, Vahid froze.

For all the...

A child danced in the streets—whirling madly in the snow. A large hood covered her features, but the ends of blonde curls poked from either side of her shoulders. She bowed and swayed, leapt and laughed in tune with the music pouring from her violin. The music possessed her, and with it the crowd. Wide-eyed he watched her dance, certain he would never see such a sight nor hear such music outside of Paradise. The tune became livelier with each note, and with it her dance. A deep bow followed by a grand leap that sent notes careening across the crowd also sent her hood flinging off her head.

The snow poured down upon her crown of gold. The dance spun her round and round. The still lit street lamp above her illuminated a hideous face of Death with every revolution she made. Vahid ducked the sudden clamber of noise. Women screamed. Men twirled their wives away. Children cried. The little girl, oblivious to it all, played on.

Frozen in the commotion, Vahid allowed one minute for fear to knife him. In that moment he knew three things: this was no ordinary progeny, her deformity wasn't the result of any accident, and his life was about to change.

While the crowds ran in the opposite direction, he ran forward, scooping the startled child into his arms. The music abruptly stopped and her voice, as penetrating as her music rent the air, nearly stopping the snow dead in the sky. Ignoring her flailing and crazed German protests, he rushed her inside before the police came to investigate.

And they would investigate. The evidence in his arms proved Vahid's worse nightmare had come true.

Erik had returned to Paris and this time he wasn't alone.

* * * *

Even the back streets were in their own right seductive. Philippe would have given in to their allure if not for the nest of snakes in his gut. Constant worry wrung on as seconds ticked off minutes, minutes into hours and hours into days and weeks since his mother had been taken. If he knew all the whys of the matter the churning wouldn't be so great. Philippe's mind was a delicate instrument, soaking up every detail it could and storing it away for future recall. But in the matter of his family's history his details were as spotty as water on silk.

Slicking back the snow from his hair he leapt over piles of slush and quickened his pace. Leaving Simone for even a second did not sit well with him, but after three hours of her insistent pleas for something to eat, Philippe caved. A flash of his smile, a flex of a sculpted arm and an irresistible wink had made the young mademoiselle at the push-cart practically shove the breads at him. His heavily accented French and the seductive lilt he placed in it didn't hurt. At least he'd learned a few things from his father.

Blowing out of his mouth and watching his breath coat the air he fought down the urge—again—to follow his father. He crammed the bread under his arm.

I know enough of the past to know you would head to the Opera Garnier. He looked around wondering what direction it was in. *But I don't understand your passion over the thoughts of madness. It simply makes no sense.*

The idea of his father being actually mad only knotted those snakes tighter. Rounding the corner on the street where he'd left his sister, he stopped in his tracks the instant he saw the empty stoop.

"Simone?" The snow in the street had been trampled, as if a mob had gathered. Philippe's heart pounded. "Simone?"

Nothing.

He saw her tiny boot prints everywhere and one large set that led straight from the center of the fray up the steps and through the door they had been deposited on. The bread dropped to the ground along with his heart.

Two strides and one sharp butt of his shoulder had him through the door and with it his panic.

* * * *

Taking flight after flight of stairs two at time, Vahid rushed into his apartments not caring to shut the door behind him. Winded, he plunked the girl down in the center of the room and paced in circles, a myriad of curses falling from his mouth.

Wake up, wake up. This is not happening. I am dreaming this. I had too much aperitif last night.

As soon as the child hit the floor she burst away from him in a tiny explosion of feet and hair. Vahid, arms akimbo in shock, stared slack-jawed at the table she clambered upon. The girl twirled to face him. Haunting golden eyes met his green ones.

This is a nightmare, never mind a dream.

A soon as he caught his breath and stopped pacing, he studied her tip to toe. The sour taste of a tart crept its way to his throat. He swallowed his revulsion and chastised himself.

Stop, Vahid. She is just a little girl. Fate, you are a cruel servant to mark her in such a way!

He tipped his head to focus on the small scrap of face not marred by the mark of Erik. That patch of youthful skin which stretched down to a ruby pout, combined with her crown of curls, would have made for the picture of innocence. He didn't realize he stared, but clearly the child did. She shrank, one small hand wrapping over the hideous part of her face. His heart panged in pity at that simple gesture.

"No, it's all right." Gingerly, he raised his hand and pulsed the air between them. An intriguing offspring of the onset of shame was shyness, but one thing was certain, if this was Erik's child, she would not be shy.

"*Guten Tag*." She yanked him from his thoughts abruptly.

Startled, Vahid shook his head clear. Her voice had the power to melt his bones in ecstasy—a rich and unusual tone, yet at the same time it pierced him.

"Tell me little one,"—Vahid cleared his throat nonchalantly—"where might your father be?"

The girl pouted as her eyes darted to and fro. The violin pressed harder against her chest. She shook her head.

Ah, Vahid realized, *she does not speak French.*

"Get away from my sister!"

Officially a nightmare.

Vahid spun around. His first impulse was to lash out at the intruder in his doorway, but that sentence, executed in perfect French pinned him to his spot. The young man filled the space, his height dwarfing Vahid and his shoulders nearly reaching from frame to frame. He was the complete opposite of the girl on his table. As deformed as she was, the boy was perfection.

Reaching up, Vahid removed his hat and tossed it on a nearby chair.

"*Your sister*? Allah have mercy." He rubbed his face as if the action would clear his head of the idea Erik had a son.

"Allah? You are the Daroga? The Persian?"

"That all depends on who desires to know." The boy made his way toward the girl. He even moved like Erik. Vahid could feel a certain beauty and command pour out the young man's steps.

"You didn't answer my question," the boy replied.

"You didn't answer mine."

"Kidnapping is a crime you know."

"Really? Tell me young man, did you learn that from your father—"

"Daroga!"

Stopping mid-retort, the world came to a screeching halt. Vahid turned to his door, moving as if swimming through mud. To his astonishment, though he shouldn't have been, he stared face to face with the black-masked nightmare of his past. The only happy person in the room was the child bubbling like a tea kettle on the table. Erik took instant command of the room, his eyes never leaving Vahid's. He walked directly to the table and plucked up the girl, whose face lit as if it were the sun itself.

Far too comfortable for Vahid' liking, Erik sat in the hearthside chair, the child curled up in his lap. The tall youth quickly took a spot at his side completing the most bizarre family portrait Vahid had ever laid eyes on. He raised a salty eyebrow and asked the question he swore he never would.

"What are you doing here, Erik?"

"Taking my children to the fair, Daroga. Why do you think I am here?"

Erik's veneer of sarcasm was never forgotten. It had an odd way of cracking the tension in the room. Vahid approached and hesitantly extended his hand. It took a moment before their forearms clasped in a cautious truce. He hid his surprise at Erik's touch. He had forgotten how cold he was.

"Daroga,"—Erik stretched his long fingers in a gesture to the young man to his side—"my heir. Philippe Georges Marie."

Vahid looked beyond Erik's son to the snow turning to rain that lashed outside his window.

Whatever reasons you chose for naming that boy after the former Comte de Chagny, I am certain I don't want to know. Mind your tongue, Vahid. Mind your tongue! Nodding a silent greeting to the boy he looked at the child in Erik's arms.

"My daughter, Simone."

Bewildered, Vahid shook his head. "Then I am...charmed?"

Erik cocked his. "Do not expect the same of her. Simone elects not to speak much lately unless it is through the violin."

The girl had tucked the instrument under her chin and was a tapping the strings with the bow. If a violin could say it was impatient to be played, then it screamed loudly.

"Through it?"

"She has my more...expressive side."

"Delightful."

"Philippe is the genius."

The boy's eyes penetrated him to the marrow. Floored and making no attempt at hiding it any longer, Vahid raised his hands and backed away from the scene before him. "I simply am not seeing this."

"Yes, Daroga. Procreation. I discovered I rather like the process."

* * * *

A light mist fell, putting a deep chill into the evening air. Though cold and damp, Erik insisted they speak outside, safely away from the children. Dinner had been a lively event, mostly an intricate side-step of Philippe's questions, which stayed for the most part focused on the opera house. The balancing act was between Simone and her curiosity of the dark skinned man. Her music had taken on a strange, exotic feel. While Erik perched himself on the balcony railing and stared off at the warm glow of Paris, Vahid looked opposite, into flickering lights of his townhome. In the distance, Simone moved like a snake charmer, filling his house with music he hadn't heard since he left the sands of his country. How she did it, he dared not ask.

"Never would I have expected this out of you, Erik."

"I thought this is what you wanted out of me, Daroga."

"It is not a complaint. I am just surprised. It has been years since we saw each other and a great deal has come to pass in that time. This is a complete concurrence to the stories I've been hearing." He tossed the remnants of a fig into a potted tree. The seeds were unusually annoying tonight. "Seeing you with children is odd. You are the Phantom of the Opera, after all. It's...peculiar."

Very few men weren't unnerved by the night's ability to make Erik's eyes glow their yellowed hue. The daroga didn't flinch under the severity of his glare.

"I am but a man, Daroga."

There was something to his tone that made Vahid down his sarcasm. "Philippe is captivating. I hope I live long enough to see that young man's untapped genius surface. There is no doubt he has a passion for the opera house. In a much better way than you did I might add." Glancing over his shoulder he noted Erik's regard was locked in the direction of the Garnier.

"He will command a world I never knew."

Their eyes met as Vahid's brow inched up. An unfathomable statement. He followed Erik's nod back toward the townhome.

"There is not a door that will not be opened to him, no opportunity denied, no rejection whatsoever. He is perfect." Erik's voice was distant.

A small, and what Vahid perceived as a proud, smile moved across Erik's thin, misshapen lips. Never in his years had he seen the monster smile.

"And the girl?"

"What of Simone?"

"One cannot help but notice she is a bit unusual. Is she..." Vahid tapped his temple.

"Mad?"

"Not the word I was looking for, but given she is your child—"

"She is a little girl, Vahid. She likes flowers and crickets and has a fondness for night. She is capable of concepts of beauty beyond your understanding, her imagination vivid and sharp. There is genius in her as well. She has no concept of destiny or fate, of cruelty or hatred, of rejection or betrayal. No concept of the ugliness that rests in the hearts of men."

Opening his mouth, Vahid tried to interject but a fuse had been lit that clearly burned for much longer than their conversation.

"She is a little girl who understands, for now, a *compassionate* world. And it is Erik's intent to keep it that way as long Erik possibly can!"

Pursing, Vahid keep his eyes level with his house. It never was a good sign when Erik began to refer to himself in third person. The monster of madness woke and was rumbling to the surface. Erik's voice shook the potted palms, yet Vahid remained unmoved.

"You great booby! How dare you pass judgment?" Erik slammed a fist into the railing. It shook behind their backs. "How dare you accuse my child of being mad?" Only when Vahid raised his hand in defeat did Erik take a deep breath and soften his tone. He himself sounded much like a wounded child. "She is the very beat of my heart, Daroga."

Erik turned away as a flare of light below them broke the night. He watched the lamplighter in silence until Vahid found his voice.

"And your companion, Mademoiselle Barret? Is she aware—"

"She knows everything of me, and it will remain that way."

Vahid shuffled in his spot. "If she is aware of your past, then mercy find all of you." He turned to regard Paris along with Erik and pressed his forearms against the cold railing. "Over several years I've been contacted by Inspector Jules Legard. He is Chief of Security for the Chagny estate now. There is quite a manhunt going on for you."

"Well aware, thank you."

"You apparently murdered some men?"

"Man."

"That's not what the authorities say. They claim you killed three people and burned down the opera's carriage house."

"Anna's father, Richard Barret, killed the managers Laroque and Wischard. I saved Anna *and* Christine by killing Barret, delight that it was, and *she* burned down the carriage house." Erik shot him a challenging look. "She stole the comte's stallion too."

"May I know why?"

"It involved Barret's kidnapping of Christine."

"Ah. That would explain the Comte de Chagny's passion in finding you. He assumes you were involved in that. Given your penchant for kidnapping Christine." Erik's posture told Vahid he wasn't amused. "So this goes beyond the death of Philippe de Chagny. France seems determined to bring you to justice for that."

Erik's golden eyes flared wide at the mention of that name. "I did not kill Philippe de Chagny!"

"I'm on your side, Erik!" Vahid bucked off the railing and stepped back. "I know your involvement with him. You both had me unwillingly entwined in your strange relationship from the start. You've no idea how far this has reached do you? This goes beyond France. They've dug deep, Erik, very deep, arming themselves with whatever they can. It's more than just chandeliers and Opera Houses. It's your very existence! Mark my words, they are obsessed with finding you. They will tear this country and any other country apart if they have to."

"They have done a lousy job thus far."

"Then why are you here?"

The remark sobered Erik instantly. Any brooding hatred Vahid detected in him throughout the night seemed for one second to fall aside.

"I came for help, Daroga. Even a man such as I can admit to needing that. I cannot saunter to Chagny, nor can I storm their mansion here. Last I did I recall nearly getting shot. A wanted man can do little to protect his kin if he is chained. But I know they are behind this." The breeze caught Erik's cloak and fluttered it behind him. "If they have her and she breaks free, she knows where I would go. What was I to do? Stay in Germany?"

"Then I'll keep their questions away as long as I can. I suggest you keep a low profile. You need to be prepared for this to catch up with you."

"Let it catch up with me. I merely will not allow them to catch up with my family. Keep my children, Daroga."

Before Vahid could question, Erik vaulted over the edge of the balcony, skimming down its walls like a black spider. Vahid whipped his head back toward the house before folding himself over the railing

"Erik, you can't leave me with children! Where are you going?"

"Where do you think, Daroga? Until I find Anna, you said it best. I am the Phantom of the Opera."

Chapter Nine

If it would have helped his impatience, Vahid would have yanked the sun up the following morning with his bare hands. Trying to explain why the best route into the opera house was via the Paris sewer system gave him a thrumming headache. Was he to saunter through the front door with two fair-skinned and phantomesque children in tow? His only option was his old tried and true route. The happy spirit of sunlight had disappeared the farther the earth swallowed them. He wasted no time that morning in following though on the decision he made the instant Erik left. He would return his two charges back to their rightful spot.

Keep his children! He is as mad as the day we parted in Persia. With Inspector Legard breathing down my neck constantly, how am I to suddenly keep two children secret especially when one is rather unpredictable? I am a withering, lonely old man, you blithering idiot. Shoving your children at me is marking us with a bull's-eye.

Moving stealthily through the abysmal corridors, he grimaced every time the youth at his side cursed in German and assaulted cobwebs. Dank passages and squealing rats seemed not to Philippe's liking. Vahid clamped his teeth.

Perhaps the lad's tastes take after his nobler namesake.

It was the little one that truly worried him. Simone seemed in her glory, tearing back her hood and gliding through the dark with what he could only describe as finesse. She poked her curly head round every corner they came by, her strange eyes blaring an intense shade of gold.

Vahid's skull split.

Out of the corner of his eye he saw her slide toward a shadow like liquid mercury. Lunging for her, he came up empty but she did not. One artful pounce had her clutching a cricket in her free hand. Shouting in delight, she shoved it toward his face.

"*Ein Abendlied!*"

Vahid recoiled. "Pardon?"

Philippe pushed past them and made an annoyed gesture. "An *Abendlied*," he parroted in a mockingly immature voice.

Patience wearing thin, Vahid rubbed his temple. "Say again?"

"Abendlied. A lullaby...an evening song?"

Vahid furrowed his brow more.

Philippe sighed. "Daroga, listen to her cricket."

Simone uncurled her fist one finger at a time to present Vahid with her miniature Maestro.

"Well,"—he grimaced—"that is one composer who will no longer be conducting."

Philippe took his sister's hand and flicked the smashed cricket aside. He stroked her palm against his trousers, wiping away the gooey remains. "She has my father's murderous side," he rumbled.

"Lovely child."

"Then you are aware."

Vahid pushed past Philippe, biting down hard on his loose tongue, his headache growing bigger than all the cellars combined. "I'm aware of what?"

"That my father is a murderer."

Vahid stopped dead, as did Philippe. Simone tore past, strings of happy German bubbling out of her mouth. They had arrived at the base of the lake, a gigantic, private pond in a dark and mysterious world.

"What exactly are you asking of me?" He followed the boy's eyes as he stared at the eerie blue light dancing above the water.

"I'm asking for the answers my father refuses to give me about the Phantom of the Opera. No great Parisian Maestro enters an opera house via a sewer unless his past is more unsavory than I suspect."

Hands on his hips, Philippe looked every bit as imposing as his father. Silent, Vahid listened.

"I know all about his blasted manhunt and how we came to be involved in it now," Philippe growled in disgust, his voice echoing through the corridor. "I will kill who took my mother with my own hands. I know my parents are innocent in the crimes that started this farce, and my father was some Phantom everyone thinks is mad, but any atrocities committed were for the sake of saving Christine Daaé."

There wasn't a pipe of opium long enough to ease Vahid's pounding temples.

"What I can't figure out is why, if he is innocent, you are taking us to him via a rat infested sewer unless there is something more to this manhunt and to him, to which I am not privy."

Saved by the blonde blur out of the corner of his eyes, Vahid turned around as Simone gleefully charged forward.

The water!

Moving with lightning speed, he hooked her into his arms before she had a chance to set foot in the frigid depths. Their bodies did an artful pirouette away from danger. He clung to her and ignored her flailing protests as he willed himself to breathe. He suspected simple country children were excellent swimmers, but not in this water...not with what mysteries he remembered it commanded.

"That," he spat, shoving a thumb toward the lake, "is what you don't know." He nodded them in the direction of the Communard road and away, he hoped, from the past. "We'll enter this way, through the third cellar." Vahid set Simone down, watching with an odd sort of relief as she darted up the road, violin under her chin, her lively notes lighting up a place of eternal darkness.

"What don't I know? Did he kill someone else?" Philippe's inquiry slapped Vahid in the back snapping the one nerve he had left.

If the children were his charges until he found Erik—then so be it. He would do as he saw fit.

Vahid turned.

Their eyes locked in a battle worthy of heaven versus earth.

There was no going back now.

"Did he kill someone else?" Vahid nodded calmly. "Where shall we start? The assassin he was for the Sultana of Persia and all the political murders he committed? With a fallen chandelier and the poor concierge that died beneath it, or perhaps with Philippe Georges Marie, the Comte de Chagny? Did he kill him or not? Maybe he tried to—the first attempt!"

The silence that followed was a blissful tonic to Vahid's pounding head.

* * * *

Twisting the children more times than a rat in a maze, Vahid breathed apprehensively as they emerged from shadow into Erik's inner sanctum. Mildew and neglect met his nose and made it crinkle. Remnants of Erik's unpredictable wrath lay strewed around the room. It wasn't the unusual house he remembered of years ago, but it still held the same sense of blood-chilling stillness. The instinct every man has to protect caused him to clamp Simone's shoulders, holding her back as Philippe cautiously stepped forward. Whatever conflicting emotions surged in the boy's head after what Vahid told him was anyone's guess. The sheer magnitude of his expression bespoke of a rising storm.

"Where are we?" Philippe harshly whispered. "Where is my father?"

Vahid kept his focus on Simone. The house made trepidation crawl up his spine like a long dead spider resurrected, and it settled on the back of his neck where it kept twitching. The monster could be anywhere in the uncharted bowels of the theater. He held Simone's shoulders and pressed her to his legs. She hopped in an excited way doing all she could to pop out of his hands.

"Is this some sort of jest? You don't mean to tell me my father *lived* here?"

Vahid remained stoic, as Philippe made a circumspect inspection of his father's past. The youth wandered amongst broken furniture and peered around corners into other rooms. His face was twisted when he left the Louis-Philippe room and his gaze cast to the floor. When he spied the pedals to the organ his eyes flared to life. Vahid tried not to react when Philippe whipped his head back to him for answers. The boy crept toward the instrument as if it would burst into life at any moment. The room beyond the organ stopped him in his tracks. Philippe shoved his arm backward and pointed.

"What...why...what kind of perverse joke is this, Daroga? Why is a coffin down here?"

"Come away from there, Philippe."

The voice, gentle as a bleating lamb, swirled around the room as if in search of its Sheppard. Philippe turned around just as Erik emerged from shadow. He took form from the darkness, a parchment in one hand, his other reaching toward Simone. Small flicks of his bony fingers beckoned his daughter to him. Vahid held fast as soon as he felt the little girl squirm to get away.

"I'm not letting go of her until I know you're in command of all your senses, Erik."

The reply didn't rise in pitch, but instead poured out with deadly intensity. "It is not the control of my senses of which you should be wary, Daroga. It is my anger right now. How dare you bring my children here?"

"With Chagny lurking, they can't stay with me. I would have explained that last night if you had not disappeared like a Phantom."

"So you bring them *here*? Even I had the presence of mind not to."

"Why not?" Philippe's outburst sliced the room in two like a guillotine. "If this place is your past, then this is ours as well, regardless of what you try to keep from us. Mainly a certain Philippe Georges Marie, the Comte de Chagny and the other artful lies you've spun!"

Vahid gripped the child in front of him as Erik lunged forward. That name triggered tension so palpable he could have ripped it off the air. The monster leaned into his son.

"How do you know of him?"

Vahid stiffened as Philippe's eyes darted toward him. Had the boy never met his father when perched on rising madness? He heard Philippe swallow. His worry however was on Erik. A paralyzing foreboding flowed through Vahid's veins as he waited for the fraction of a second it took for the monster to explode.

"Him?" Erik pointed. "You are to believe nothing that great twit tells you! Nothing, Erik says! Nothing! It is your mother who speaks the truth of our past and how *dare* you believe the words of anyone over her?"

"Mother's story only collaborated yours. But it makes too much sense now doesn't it? The reason why Chagny pursues us so relentlessly is not because of murder in self-defense to help a nobleman's wife, and some misconstrued story about opera houses and con men, but things beyond this manhunt—*far beyond*! You *are* mad, aren't you?"

"I am not a madman!"

A low rumble came from Erik's throat as he shoved past his son. Up and down he paced as if to control a Titan growing inside of him. Vahid watched the same tension nearly shake Philippe. It was as if he looked into a strange mirror that reflected only personalities. Philippe's eyes eventually lowered and looked to his side.

Vahid sighed. *That boy loves you Erik—mad or not. He only wants to understand.* Vahid's slight nod urged Philippe to come to him, and, as the boy did Erik grabbed for his daughter and scooped her up into his long arms in one deft motion.

"Believe what you wish. I am numb to it all," Erik admitted. "Keep your head, Philippe, lest the sins of the father become the sins of the son. We are not mad."

"If that is the case, then prove it. Let me help." Philippe's voice was a thin, but passionate whisper.

Vahid lifted a brow. *Prove it? Bold words for such a youth, but I disagree.* "I can only do so much, Erik, but do not involve your son in this. I implore you." He chose his words with caution, ceasing to breathe as Erik raised his hands to his mask.

The monster lowered it and tossed it to a table. Vahid hitched his breath and felt pressure grip his chest. It had been years since he had seen the supreme ugliness of the Opera Ghost unmasked.

Reaching out, Erik tenderly lowered the hood that cloaked Simone's face. This time a mirror of a different sort was present and Vahid couldn't help but stare aghast at father and daughter.

"No masking this face anymore," Erik said numbly. "She will never be made to suffer."

The monster came toward them, his strange eyes filled with an intensity making Vahid wonder if he was capable of reading souls. Erik held out the parchment. Neatly folded and franked with a macabre seal, Vahid's eyes slapped on the name on the front. He refused to take it. There were limits to what he was willing to do in servitude to the Phantom.

"Not again Erik. Don't start in with your infernal notes."

Philippe took it instead and inwardly Vahid cursed. The boy asked no questions and made no comments, rather lowered the brief to his side and stared at his father with all the seriousness of a time-hardened man. One way or another Philippe was determined to gain access to his entire father even if being his advocate was the way to do so.

Erik spoke to his son.

"Leave with the Persian. Have him escort you to the post and see that is mailed. If I cannot go to the comte, the man can come to me. I am certain he will seek me out once he reads that. The boy is predictable."

There wasn't a single sweet cloud of smoke that could numb the alliance Vahid watched form before his eyes. Philippe merely wanted his mother back and Erik his family intact. What right had he to judge? Were they all not servants to the truth and the truth often attended by danger? A light came back to Philippe's eyes. Vahid didn't like it.

As if Erik read his mind, he spoke. "Daroga, I have behaved long enough."

The melancholy playing of a violin tripped Vahid's thoughts away from anything else. Distilled in those achingly confused notes were the reasons he kept his silence and slowly allowed himself to be written into the Phantom's opera once again.

Through the violin a little girl wept tears only a mother could soothe.

Chapter Ten

Her heart still raced, making Christine hotter than comfortable.

How? How could you do this to me, Raoul? She stared at the doors to the salon, mentally preparing to go inside. *How can that woman be in my home and not an appropriate prison? How can he permit this injustice to the Chagny name?*

The two burly footmen stationed on either side didn't give her a glance, and if they had, Christine would have leveled them with one of her own—just as she did her husband after letting him know how displeased she was to discover where Anna Barret was. *In my home!* Subconsciously her hands fluttered about her dress as if preparing to meet a queen, not her nemesis.

I will not let her see my nerves.

Inwardly she felt small and low. It wasn't Raoul's fault that woman was here, but Loup's, and Christine was powerless against *him*.

Swallowing the fear Loup's name evoked, she breathed deeply and laid a hand on the knob.

I'll heed Raoul's suggestion to leave for a spell and take some time away from the house to shop Paris and enjoy the World's Fair...after I know. After Mademoiselle Barret looks me in the eye. After I pry and scrutinize and see if she knows where Erik may be. I must know of him. I must!

Keeping his name tucked under her heart, she twisted the knob and glided into the sun-filled salon. As the door closed behind her, Christine scanned the room, spying Anna staring out a window to the courtyard below.

"Mademoiselle Barret," she addressed, somehow knowing the woman wouldn't pay her the appropriate respect and address her first. "We meet again."

When she turned, Christine's heart leapt to her throat.

Merciful God! The shades of green and purple on her cheek would turn tender any stomach. Christine swallowed and forced herself to continue. "Your tenure at my home is only by the graces of my husband. You will be sent to prison soon, I'm told. I can't say this upsets me, given what you have placed my family through over the years."

"I've placed your family through nothing. Any perpetuation of this affair is due to your lies, as you are aware."

Indignant, Christine took a few steps toward her and stopped. "How dare you. You cannot speak for me." She followed Anna's steady gaze toward the courtyard and the carriage that waited. Her eyes were locked on André as he patiently stood near the team.

"Is he yours?" Anna asked quietly.

Caught off guard, Christine watched her son momentarily before discovering a distant and sad look in Anna's eye. "That is my son. André Thaddeus Marie, the Vicomte de Chagny. He just turned sixteen."

"Quite the man already."

The frankness to her voice put rocks in Christine's churning stomach making her entire body feel heavy. She jutted her chin to the ceiling and tried to ignore them. "I would appreciate it if you did not speak of my son. I'm well aware of the murder you committed against the house of Molyneaux and I will not have the likes of your eyes upon my child." As a puff of air broke through Anna's lips, Christine laid a hand on her tumbling rocks and quickly changed the subject. "My husband has informed me you've been alone. That you have no idea where Erik is and you haven't seen him in years."

Anna turned. "I haven't."

Lie or truth? Christine couldn't tell. "I can't say that surprises me, Mademoiselle Barret. Erik never would have followed you after that fire. The Phantom goes where he goes." Christine's voice dipped in tone betraying her sadness, yet she took pity at the look that flared behind Anna's eyes. Seeing it gave her a renewed courage and strength. She took her hand off the rocks in her belly.

"You threw your life away praying for his love. Helping him escape the opera house, thinking he would return that favor and love you. I hope you have not wasted these years thinking on why you did that. You could never have understood the depth of the Angel of Music and how he loves. Not as completely as I do."

Anna nodded out the window toward André. "Is he his?"

Christine's eyes shot open. "Of course not!"

Anna turned back to the window, her tone spitting bullets through the windowpane. "Then I will stand here and remember with a silent and private satisfaction the passion involved the night *your* Angel of Music created *my* son."

Frozen by the implication, Christine stood as strong and unyielding as the footmen on guard outside.

You lie. You are definantly lying! I know! I feel it my core. The Angel of Music is more than mere man. He...he...is an immortal presence rooted in my soul. Not yours! Erik would never take another under his wing. He would never have chosen you. Never!

"You speak wicked lies, Mademoiselle. Erik is not a man! He is far, far more and untouchable by any mortal soul. You seek to vindictively destroy him for some reason like you do my family. Stand there and be as you are and refuse to tell us of his whereabouts, it matters not. Your association with him ends with a carriage to Belgium where you can take your lies with you."

"My association ends? So long as my son lives and breathes the very essence of the man you so ardently claim to be yours...so long as my *daughter* sees the world though the golden eyes of her father and the fair-haired curls that were my mother's, my association with him will never end. Erik is *my* inspiration, *my* blessing and *my* soul, and I would appreciate it if you did not speak of *my children*. I am well aware of the lies *you* committed against the house of Chagny to perpetuate your ridiculous jealousy, and I will not have you wish for one moment longer that Erik is any part of *you!*"

Christine stared at her so stonily she thought her heart too heavy to resume beating. "Liar! This will all be over soon." She backed toward the door. "As soon as you are gone and locked away forever, everything will be as it was."

Christine fumbled with the doorknob and gasped when it finally sprung open, giving her freedom. She didn't look back once and barely acknowledged the servants tending to her cloak and bonnet. She fled through the halls, out the door, and to the courtyard below and didn't stop until her shaking hand was resting in the strong grip of her son. Only once he assisted her into the coach did she look up toward the salon window.

Anna's silhouette would haunt her almost as much as her untruths.

* * * *

Headaches put Raoul in a foul mood, especially when they assaulted him first thing in the morning. The aroma of fine grapes stung his nostrils as he poured two fingers of cognac. Maybe it would dull the pounding. What didn't was the knocking on his library door.

What now? "Enter!"

He needed interruptions? Christine's displeasure rattled him enough. When his wife wished it, she could hit notes in protest that could shatter eardrums. Whoever was about to disturb his peace would get the brunt of his ill humor. He presented the footman bowing respectfully in the doorway with his best nailing look, before slamming the crystal cap back on the decanter.

"Let him in."

The Persian wasn't exactly a sight for sore eyes. "Daroga, to what do I owe the pleasure? Are you here with news, or merely seeking a morning libation out of the eyes of critics?" He scooped up his glass, drank deep, winced, and slammed his snifter down. "Actually, Daroga, ignore that inquiry and just tell me why you are here. It has been a long morning already."

"I always did enjoy the Chagny civility," the Persian replied drolly.

Raoul folded an arm across his chest and perched his elbow on a fist. The other loomed before his left cheek. An invisible block to an impromptu meeting he wanted nothing to do with presently. He had a fugitive in his salon and a less than sane bounty hunter stinking up his halls. He moved his fist hand, punching the words away in a silent command for his guest to keep talking.

"Before I begin, tell me," the dark man inquired, "where is your wife?"

The brow Raoul hitched lifted a notch higher than his patience. "She is out for the day enjoying the fair. So if you wish to speak with her, leave your card. I have a matter at hand I don't want her subjected to."

"I should say." The Persian slid a note toward him. "I have little idea where that came from or who delivered it, but that seal and red-ink are unmistakable. It appeared on my desk when I woke this morning. Beyond this I have nothing additional for you."

The Persian kept blinking. Why couldn't he keep his focus? He was hiding something, perhaps even lying. It burned in Raoul more than the cognac and oddly written note. Its sloppy strokes, as if the author never learned to join his letters, studied him back like the jaws of a serpent poised to strike. Unfolding, it he read aloud.

Fondest greetings, Monsieur le Comte:

My sincerest regards to you. I hope the years have brought you the best in comfort and respect. That being said, the pleasantries of this note end here. Your endless pursuit of me has drawn to a close and I request your audience. I will be frightfully blunt for I find it rather suits me, and though I am an enemy of scandal there is no avoiding what is about to befall you. You should know by now it is best not to raise my temper.

Raoul's gaze tightened as he looked from the note to its messenger.

It is for the sake of the innocent that I barely keep my temper in check. If you ever wished to know how to anger me, you have found out.

Heed my warning. Proceed with caution, Monsieur. You have toyed with my heirs.

Ph. of the O.

It took a few seconds to register the signature, the scarlet ink, the matchstick-like scrawl and the tone of the note. The icy wave that jerked Raoul's spine sobered him the instant his glare punched the Persian.

"Where is he? At the Garnier?"

"I took the liberty to search the Garnier. It is as you left it years ago."

"Perhaps, or you've been lying and covering for him." He slapped the letter down on the blotter. "This simply *appeared* on your desk? Do you take me for a fool? Where is he?" A lack of patience made the muscles around his right eye jump.

"Moreover than that, where is Mademoiselle Barret?" The Persian's tone was one only a former investigator could summon. "He cares little over where your wife is apparently. You should worry on her and take care to keep the two separate."

As if Raoul didn't know that and hadn't spent the morning flaying himself for permitting Anna to sit like a target in his salon. "Why come here and advise me of this if you don't have any information?" The adrenaline filling him took excellent care of curbing his rising headache.

"I'm only doing as you wish of me, Monsieur."

"Mademoiselle Barret is here." Raoul ground his teeth together as if chewing back his words. The Persian scrutinized him. There was something behind his jade eyes, like a spark of recognition. The man would be a horrible poker player.

"Keeping Mademoiselle Barret here is fodder for L'Epoch if word ever gets out. How did you come by her?"

"I'm well aware of L'Epoch. I sent Loup to Germany awhile back with instructions to uncover whatever he could. I was not expecting Anna Barret to arrive on my *doorstep*." Raoul reached for the cognac again. "Her maddening silence, coupled with my wife's displeasure, could make me a drunkard if I didn't find such despicable." He gestured with the drink. "You can blame my demandable conscience for her tenure here. Regardless of her crimes, I can't look beyond the fact that she is a woman. I can't see women in prison, at least not on my head. Once in Belgium it will be out of my hands. She has suffered enough." The bruising on the girl's face came to mind with his next sip.

"You intend to bring Mademoiselle Barret to Brussels?"

"Such is the only solution at this point. I intend to make the arrangements this afternoon. I cannot keep her here until she confesses what she knows—L'Epoch you know." Raoul smiled sarcastically. "She is uncooperative. Let the Brussels authorities close of this one unsavory chapter in my life. My huntsman can deal with her from now on." Warming his drink with his palm, Raoul shook his head. The insufferable intolerance he had for his bounty hunter had gnawed at him through the years. Loup had been a necessary and often uncontrollable evil.

"From what I know his methods are unorthodox and often immoral. Are you mad? Release her custody to me. Perhaps I can get her to talk."

Raoul lowered his glass. The cognac did little but rot him from the inside out anyway. "Truly? What cares have you if she is here or in Brussels for justice? Unless you know where Erik is and your outrage is a result of some misplaced loyalty to him and the girl?"

"I have interrogated men for far more years than any of you. She won't speak to you because you are the enemy, Monsieur."

Raoul lifted the note and tapped it on the desk before gesturing to the door with it. "We shall see about that. I have the upper hand now, and am going to use it. Perhaps this note and a shock to her system will make her talk."

* * * *

Anna tripped over the length of her skirts as Loup hauled her through the halls. Flanked on her other side by Legard, she forced herself to stare forward. She was getting dizzy volleying her head between the two. They had come for her out of nowhere, abruptly plucking her from her the salon to hasten her through the maze of the massive townhome. They ended within the comte's private library. He stood center of the ornate room, his expression less than pleasant. To his side was a man she hadn't seen in years, but whose jade eyes were as unmistakable as Erik's golden ones.

The Persian!

Anna forced her attention away from him lest the recognition flicker on her face.

"Am I to assume you still have nothing to say?" Raoul strode forward.

Looking from him to the Persian, she caught the slight flare to his eye that bid her to hold her tongue.

"I told you all I know, Monsieur."

He extended a note. "Go on. Read it. Your friend over here—" he gestured to the Persian—"delivered that. I suspect you two know each other?"

93

Anna stared at the page. It took all her might not to yank her face away from those scarlet letters and look toward the center of Paris. She shook her head denying she knew the dark man and prayed the lie didn't dance on her face.

"You have lied to me, Mademoiselle," Raoul said.

Anna's neck cramped. She let the page fall to her side and lifted her shoulders in a careless shrug. "I know not your exotic looking friend. I told you I've not seen Erik in years." The note crunched loudly as she handed it back to him. "And what makes you think I can read?"

Inside, her belly churned. She *could* read and Erik was angry—violently so. But he was here. Why had he sought the Persian? Were they to be allies? Did he know where Erik was? Certain Erik's madness was on the rise, the desperation to make it to his side and their children's threatened to make her explode.

"Nothing you say matters any longer, Mademoiselle. Since you have been uncooperative you're heading to Belgium. There are crimes you've committed there and will meet justice for. All I need to know is in that letter anyway."

"Belgium?" She glanced, horror struck at the Persian. Could all read the panic no doubt on her face?

"Scaring the accused rarely works, Monsieur le Comte. I think you are better off keeping the Mademoiselle here."

Anna bit her tongue. The Persian had elaborated the last word and locked eyes with her. *Erik is here! Where are my children? I must get to the Garnier. Where else would he go?*

"Again you judge me by my name alone without seeing any other side than that which you want to see." Anna played off the Persian's lead. "I have no business in Belgium anymore than I do here."

"No, Mademoiselle. I judge by the past, the only definition by which man should be judged. Once in Belgium the authorities will take it from there. That is unless you have certain information that may help me settle my affairs here."

Anna thought she registered a twitch to his upper lip that made his fine blond moustache jump. Nerves perhaps? She made certain any concern didn't resurrect on her face.

"I told you all I know. I haven't seen Erik in years."

She had to keep her association with Erik secret. She bit her cheek until she nearly tasted blood. *How am I to do that after my confession and outburst with the comtess? She knows I have children by Erik. She will relay that information if she has not already!* Anna prayed this was all some elaborate trick to toy with her mind. She had to get out of there.

"I suspect this entire thing is a ploy on your behalf to get me to speak," she assumed. "Anyone can pen a note to you and claim it to be from the Phantom, Monsieur le Comte. I'm afraid you have built quite the reputation."

Patience having snapped, he jerked his head over his shoulder, indicating door. "Take her. Ready a carriage for Belgium."

"Monsieur le Comte," the Persian bid as Legard and Loup wedged themselves around her. "You are going about this the wrong way and must appeal to a woman's natural instinct."

"What would *that* be, Daroga?"

"She claims she cannot read. I believe her. So we inform her that the note mentions heirs. Have you children, Mademoiselle?"

The Persian had weighed her down with a heavy look. Anna searched around her as if perplexed by it all.

"You need not answer." He turned to the comte. "Give her time alone to reflect on that and perhaps she will spill all. There is no telling what could happen to orphaned children, after all."

Anna caught the near imperceptible nod of his head. He was trying to keep her from Brussels. Biding time.

"It is either you think on that, Mademoiselle, and what could happen to your family or you return to Brussels never giving them an opportunity for a voice," the Persian warned.

Anna opened her mouth to speak but was cut short

"Will you all just learn how to handle a woman and be done with this? Beat it out of her!" Loup's hand cut through the air and contacted with stinging force against her cheek.

Before she could even cry from the pain, or acknowledge the resulting shout of protests from Legard and the Persian, the comte rounded. Like a shot from a catapult his fist smashed the side of Loup's jaw flattening the bounty hunter to the floor. He grabbed him by the collar and brought their faces inches apart.

"I will not have any women abused as a result of this. Get yourself under control in regard to her or I swear you will not walk away from his manhunt intact."

Loup writhed on the ground, his face purple with fury. Anna backed away, her hand against her heated cheek. She searched the Persian's eyes for what to expect next.

"Monsieur le Comte, though you act in all good honor, you are a complete and utter fool." The Persian stood boldly at Anna's side. He locked a hand around her upper arm. She gasped and looked from him, to Raoul, to Legard and finally down to the rising rage on Loup's face.

"Angering a man like Loup, then sending her off with him will only kill her," the Persian pointed out. Anna felt a slight pressure to her upper arm as if signaling to her that he was using the situation to her advantage. "Didn't you just regret the abuse she has already endured?"

Anna's eyes flew open in shock. The comte had—sympathy toward her?

"Regret?" Loup growled, bolting to his feet. He lunged toward Raoul, his voice thundering like an angry stallion let loose. "*Regret*? You miserable dog. I do what you want and you dare *regret* how I manage this manhunt? No one regrets my services! I am the best bloody huntsman in Europe!" Loup rounded on Anna, grabbing her opposite arm and hauling her out of the Persian's grip.

"What do you think you are doing?" Raoul blocked Loup's path.

"Taking what is mine and leaving you and your pathetic investigators to draw this hunt to a close on their own." He shoved his chin in the direction of Legard and the Persian. "I've waited long enough for Anna Barret and waiting here for all of you to make up your mind tries my patience. It is time I gather my prize and be done with you. No amount of money is as delightful as riding Anna to Belgium *my* way. I am not about to let you keep her here while you dance around tracking down your Phantom. Any idiot would just go to the opera house, put a bullet in his head and be done with it by now."

"We don't know for certain he is there," Raoul shouted. "Mademoiselle Barret—"

"Could be your perfect bargaining chip if you had a single ounce of man in your spine," Loup snarled. He pointed an imaginary gun to Anna's temple. "You want your little ghost, you merely reply to his note and tell him you have his whore at the end of steel and see how fast he comes running. Or perchance you are too afraid that your wife will go running *toward* him and not away from him?"

"Enough! Restrain him!"

Raoul's sharp command shattered the air around them. In the blink of an eye Legard was on Loup, pinning his arms behind his back. The sudden move tumbled Anna to the side and into the Persian. His whisper was as soft and as fast as Hermes.

"Keep your mouth shut on what you know, but play the worried mother. Anything to keep the comte from sending you off. He is sympathetic toward women. I think he will hold you here. I will inform Erik and your children you are safe and will stall Chagny all I can. Monsieur le Comte," he said loudly. "What is it you intend to do? Anger that huntsman further?"

"Get him out of here," Raoul growled to Legard. "I am done with him. His tenure his over. Mademoiselle Barret will remain in Chagny custody until she tells me what I want to know—for the sake of her children." He arched a brow.

The Persian slightly shook her arm to prove his plan was in motion.

"You deny me Anna? Deny me what is mine?" Loup bucked in Legard's grip shouting at Raoul as he was hauled toward the doors. "Burn in hell you shit! I play by my rules and will have what is mine!" Sharply butting Legard with his shoulder, he freed himself and tapped his temple with that imaginary pistol. "This is far from over now."

Anna leaned into the Persian's grip attempting to back away from Loup as he propelled himself toward the streets of Paris, cursing all the way.

Chapter Eleven

"I am beginning to understand why you avoided this place."

Thumbing his watch back in his pocket for the third time, André eyed the filling theater unenthusiastically. In the past the opera rejuvenated him despite the mysterious stigma of the Phantom lurking around his parents. Now, knowing all the facts and how they tied in with his beloved uncle, the Chagny box at the Garnier proved suffocating.

"André, I am not happy in the least of your father's decisions, but what is done is done." His mother laid a hand on his arm, preventing him from removing his watch again. "If I could have kept this all from you forever I would have. I don't like Mademoiselle Barret being under our noses either, but we must respect how your father handles this. Once done, let's hope the opera will still bring happy memories."

André stared down at the curtain as they waited for the second act. Taking his mother out on the town had done little to calm his jitters. She seemed distracted the entire coach ride. He drove with her along the Seine watching the morning sun wane to afternoon, pampered her over a lunch, assisted her in purchasing a new pearl necklace and took a carriage ride through the Boise, all along listening to her laugh and claim how like his father he was.

Highly unlikely that I am like him. I would have ended this farce years ago by killing the Phantom the instant opportunity arose.

The notes of musicians warming up swirled around them like lost disorganized bees in search of the hives upon the rooftop. Glancing to his mother, he noted the pinch to her brow. Her unusual calm was another well-performed stage trick. Unlike her, he couldn't bear to sit in the theater one minute longer.

"I will return. I need a bit of air before act two."

As soon as the door to the box closed behind him he shot his breath out his mouth. Never had this lifelong manhunt affected him so. He needed to walk off his anxiety before stress aged him so badly no lady would ever pass an eye to him.

* * * *

He needed to walk off his anxiety before his father killed him.

"Simone," he rumbled.

If he was able to find his sister in catacombs beneath the monastery back home, why couldn't he find her in an opera house? Charged with one task of minding her and she was gone in the blink of an eye. His nostrils flared.

So I take my eyes off her to thumb through an abandoned score of my father's. Does that warrant this death sentence?

His father did little but pace in those infernal vaults they now called home. The Daroga was no help. He escorted Philippe as far as the post that morning, only to decide not to permit him to post the letter, but deliver it himself. Philippe was deposited back at the sewer they had originally entered by as the Persian left.

I should have delivered that letter. Philippe punched his thigh in frustration. It was *he* who wanted to assist his father. *I am a man in this, not a child! When will they all understand that?*

But here he was instead, getting lost in a maze playing keeper to Simone's unpredictability again. Philippe was unwilling to enter the depths of the theater again when the Persian left him, but he did anyway.

Doesn't my sheer determination prove me a man? It took everything he had to press forward and retrace their steps himself. The longer he missed his mother the angrier he became. The more he thought on the strange transformation of his father the more confused he was. Having Simone disappear was the last thing he needed.

It is not my fault if my sister tends to be a bit unhinged of late. "Simone!"

Philippe attempted to keep to corners and shadows, though he felt like the limelight was flaring at his feet. He couldn't be more terribly out of place. The theater was in full swing for the evening with well-dressed people of a clearly higher class roaming everywhere. Wherever *everywhere* was. He was utterly lost. Just the thought of that made his skin pebble.

The least my father could have done was to give me some orientation to this maze instead of sitting in silence when not pacing. Mein Gott!

That was to say when Philippe knew where his father was. He slipped in and out of his sight more than once. Philippe had been covering the grounds of this opera house for hours—the halls, the streets, everywhere looking for his sister.

Not wanting to stand out in his simpler country garb, he picked up his pace and rounded a corner full stride. "Simone, I swear when I get my hands on you I am going to—*Gott!*"

"*Dieu!*"

The collision slammed him and his additional expletives flat on his back. Air burst out of his lungs with a hot, strangled moan as he stared star-struck at a giant chandelier above him. If he hit a column, a mirror, or person he knew not. Shaking his head clear, he realized it was the latter when a hand shot down to him.

"I beg your pardon, Monsieur. I should have been paying mind to what was in front of me and not the time."

Looking beyond an elaborate signet, up the forearm of the finest eveningwear he ever seen, Philippe locked eyes with a youth his age.

"Pay it no mind," he muttered, clasping the forearm and rising.

"You're not injured? I would assume it would take more than a fall to marble to hurt one of the Garnier's stagehands, but what are you doing out here?"

Stagehand? Philippe scowled and brushed his trousers, a useless gesture, for the Garnier's floors were so clean a surgeon would be at home. Although such inquiry was a natural assumption given his attire. "I am not a stagehand, Monsieur." What was he supposed to tell him? This was a nobleman before him and his tone insisted Philippe answer. Not used to speaking with nobility of any sort, he scrubbed the back of his neck. "Ah...my ahhh...sister darted in here to get out of the rain. Yes, the rain! I appear to have lost her in the maze of halls. I implore you not to call the authorities. I shall be on my way as soon as I locate her."

"For Lord's sake why would I do that? Every man has a right to duck out of this abysmal Paris weather. Come." He pointed down a corridor. "We shall let the management know and every available hand will search for her."

"That's really not—"

"No arguments. Her age?" They began to walk.

"Seven."

He extended his hand. "A child! Too young to be on her own. We pick up our pace. Perhaps this is a bit forward of our acquaintance so soon, but I am nothing if not a bit unconventional. You may call me André."

Philippe accepted and offered his name as well as Simone's when asked for it.

"I detect an accent to your French. German is it?"

Philippe nodded, being put at easy by André's friendly presence. "This is my first time to Paris. My sister gets a bit overly excited, I'm afraid."

"First time? You don't say? Here for the fair are you? My mother is a Prima Donna. She studied and sang here."

Philippe tripped over his feet and nearly met the floor again. Utter amazement filled every facet of his mind. An insatiable musical curiosity peaking...

André casually tugged on the sleeves of his waistcoat and turned them down another corridor. "This opera house has been a part of my family for generations."

Philippe bit his tongue. When had he ever been jealous? Growing up around monks it was hardly an emotion he explored. He was tempted to best André by blurting out that his Maestro of a father had much to do with the facility also.

"Is your father a hand here as well?" André questioned cheerfully.

However, small talk wasn't exactly what Philippe desired right now and frankly the answer to that question was a clear-cut no. "My father is a carpenter." It was almost impossible to keep the disdain of that sentence off his tongue.

As if on cue, Philippe's short words served as a divide between their classes. André went silent. Wandering down the hall did more and more to unsettle Philippe. Passing by floor to ceiling mirrors, they were a complete contradiction—André the picture of nobility, Philippe the picture of...what? He refused to look into a mirror to find out. In Germany he knew who he was. Erik's son who lived at the monastery and delighted in doing anything he could for the benefit of the monks with an occasional jaunt to do anything he could for the frauleins of the village. The music in him was a sleeping mystery. Here it cracked open like a roaring monster. The opera house was the most fantastic place he had ever been and the one man who could lay a world of music at his feet was ensconced in its bowels like some perverse nightmare. The vestibule they were in opened to an opulent entry and he stared in wonder at the Grand Escalier.

Amazing!

Drawn to the details like a bee to honey, he couldn't help but rotate in his spot. How he longed to run his hand along the detailed columns. Lifting a brow he studied the scantily clad female sculptures that held aloft the gaslights. He approached the three staircases when his daydream came to a crashing halt.

"This way, Monsieur. Patrons only up those stairs." André pointed down an empty hall.

Philippe swallowed his disappointment which ended in a choking cough as soon as he heard the music.

"Blast." He checked his guide. André heard the music too and before it grew any louder Philippe spun round one of the risqué lamps and dashed in its direction down the lower staircases.

He found her staring intently into an alcove beneath the lower ramps of the Escalier. Simone's head was cocked in a curious manner as she gazed at the figure of a woman with her arms outstretched as if reaching for some unknown thought or sound. Lightly tripping tones undulated off her violin. Upon seeing her brother she pointed, silencing the violin for a moment.

"Does she hear birds in her head too?" she innocently asked.

Philippe looked over his shoulder to see André jogging down the stairs. Yanking Simone's hood up, he smothered her face into his hip.

"You've found her I take it?" André said cheerfully.

"Yes, thank you kindly for your assistance, Monsieur—"

Simone's fist pummeled his hips as her violin batted him on the rump. She wiggled and squirmed out of his grip. Stripping her hood off, she peered around him. Philippe's heart stilled as she blurted the query to André.

"Does she hear birds in her head or not?"

"*Pour l'amour de Dieu!*" André stumbled backward.

Philippe sucked in his breath as the back of André's hand shot to cover his mouth. Startled, Simone raised her right hand to cage her face. She looked aghast at her brother then back to André. The alcove they stood in was just dark enough that her piercing yellow eyes shone in the shadows.

"What in the name of Christ—"

"Still your tongue now," Philippe insisted, "and speak of us to no one. She is merely a little girl."

Gathering Simone into his arms he shoved beyond his startled guide and headed down the closest corridor he could find.

"Wait," André called out behind him. "Your forgiveness, please. My shock was only natural."

Philippe cursed under his breath and quickened his stride. Blast the prejudicial world! Judgment wasn't natural. Setting his jaw he stopped when a hand on his shoulder prevented his escape. With a great pressure growing in his chest, he turned.

"Your forgiveness, please." André reached into his jacket pocket and extended a card. "Allow me to make it up to you at some—" he looked at Simone—"less pressing time."

Philippe snatched the card and crammed it in his pocket not bothering to read the name. Turning, he continued into shadows. "Some other time, perhaps."

"Might I know who may call on me, Monsieur? Your full name?"

Philippe stopped again and met the perplexed look on Simone's face. They didn't have surnames. That jealousy twisted in him again. What would he place on a calling card? Son of Erik? Glancing over his shoulder he offered all he could before hastening to any sanctuary he could find.

"Philippe Georges Marie."

Chapter Twelve

With André gone she let her shoulders droop. Act two began, but Christine gave no care to Meyerbeer. Tears leaked at her eyes as memories connecting her to the theater ran like a river through her.

Anna Barret was in custody, but where was Erik? Would he be close behind? Christine was certain Raoul would be furious at them for coming here and would want her nowhere near the theater in light of the developments. If that woman was captured, then rest assured Erik wouldn't be happy. It was only a matter of time before he showed up and then what would she do? She didn't believe for one minute Anna didn't know Erik's whereabouts. She merely rejected the thought of their children.

I can't let Erik be arrested and carted off to a certain death. But if I don't, what will they all suspect? Raoul already assumes I protect Erik, and if I admit such—our family name would be scandalized.

Christine leaned her head against her hand. It all seemed highly impossible she would ever find the answers.

The door opened. Tension redressed her shoulders as André—unusually stiff shouldered himself—sat next to her. An unshakeable sense of apprehension rose within her. Never had she seen her son so pale.

"André, what is it?"

With a finger perched across his upper lip and his elbow digging into the velvet arm of the chair he looked at her before staring emptily out across the theater. "What did the Phantom look like?"

Gooseflesh instantly claimed her skin. She stammered silently as André's other hand crushed hard the chair's arm.

"I just encountered something I wish to heaven I could tear from my eyes, for never in my life have I ever witnessed such supreme horror on any living soul."

Christine's heart lurched, while at the same time shook with anticipation none would understand.

"There is a face of Death with yellow eyes in this opera house," he whispered.

His next question twisted her spleen until she was certain all the blood was gone from her body.

"What did the Phantom look like, *Maman*?"

"He...he wore a mask of Death. A man cursed with an inhuman ugliness that radiates the very image of horror. A face that once you have seen it, it burns in your mind and nothing can eliminate what it tattoos upon your soul." The once warm pearls around her neck now felt bitterly cold. "You have seen this? He is here?"

"No."

Jolting, her heart plummeted to the floor. Was she relieved or devastated? Christine cornered her son when their eyes met.

"André, please, what do you mean?" Her face contorted, begging him to relieve her of this torture.

"What righteous God curses a little *girl* in such a manner and gives her flawless brother my *uncle's* name?"

Somewhere in the madness of her son's words, Christine felt Erik's presence in all his strength and glory—just as she had in the past. She leaned away from André, painfully conscious of how much he reflected his father. His tone had the same determination for answers as Raoul's did years ago when this manhunt began. Emotion clogging her throat, her son had given her all the answer she needed.

Erik was in Paris.

Christine rose trying to regain her composure. "Make haste and bring me home." She followed him silently out of their box praying her shaking wasn't apparent. As soon as the door closed, her trembles worsened. She gripped André for support as the theater police approached.

"Madame la Comtess, Monsieur le Vicomte. Monsieur le Comte sent us to locate you. He desires you safely back at the townhome immediately."

She nodded. "Immediately then."

Clearly Raoul knew something as well. Did she shiver from fear of what it was, or a misguided shock that Erik—of all people—had children, and that Anna Barret spoke the truth?

* * * *

"You speak the truth?" She recognized her husband's inherent authority over the situation, but that didn't stop the nerves suddenly scorching her stomach as if she swallowed a hot potion. The strains of Meyerbeer seemed like a distant memory as her family gathered in his library. Standing behind his desk, Raoul wore his resolve like never before.

"Loup's been dismissed. I shall continue to find Erik on my own. Between Chagny resources and the Paris authorities I am certain this will be at its end." Raoul nodded toward André. "I will need you in this. Do not leave your mother's side."

Christine felt worry march across her brow. "What of Mademoiselle Barret? This is Loup of which you speak. For years he had been embroiled in—"

"Are you lamenting this, Christine? The man has proven time and again to be as unstable as Erik. I'm sickened by what he has done, regardless of to whom. I know it is not a prudent move given the years he has served Chagny, but let him be gone." Raoul sliced the air with his hand. "Mademoiselle Barret is captured and we will send her on to Belgium as soon as we are able and our ties will totally be cut with Loup forever."

Fear nearly burned a hole in her throat. Flames licked the air in the hearth, mocking the fire that wrapped around her neck. Eyes locked on the orange swirls, she moved toward it wishing it was the past that would burn away.

Think!

What was she to do? Raoul's fortitude waved higher than Chagny's standard. Loup had all but delivered Erik into Paris with his capture of Anna and now, with André's perplexing sighting at the Garnier, there was no doubt Erik was here. Or...at least his kin was. She glanced over her shoulder. Her son seemed lost in it all, but he held his tongue. Finally, after so many years Erik would go to Devil's Island...to his death.

She touched the mantle. The marble was strikingly cold.

He can't be sent away. He can't! He is still the Angel of Music to me. I will do anything, Erik, to keep you at large. But how?
Faster and faster the years turned in her mind.
Loup will tell. If not paid handsomely by Raoul as in the past, he will tell him of my affections for Erik. André's future will be ruined. The pittance I pay from my allowance for his silence is not enough. Not nearly enough.

A quick glance out the window toward Paris gave her the idea. The fair was ongoing. Thousands had descended upon Paris. She could find a way, sell belongings, sell some property somehow, convince their barrister it was her husband's wish? Chagny was enormous. Perhaps...perhaps Raoul would never know? She toyed with a ring on her right hand, an elaborate emerald, one of many in her collection. Sell that? Give Loup that for now and then promise him the money from the land? Pay him double what Raoul had through the years to thwart her husband's efforts?

Whatever she did, she had to do it and do it soon.

Christine barely heard herself agreeing to her husband's decision through the blood drumming in her ears.

* * * *

Fist before his mouth, Philippe crouched with his back against a marble column. Listening to her wavering notes, he wondered if it were blessing or sickness that plagued his sister. On and on she bowed, her notes vibrating from one side of the hall to the next. They wove unseen webs capable of entrapping any who dared to wander too close. If he closed his eyes her music carried him through that web, away to levels of himself he didn't know existed. Philippe wasn't certain of anything in his life beyond wanting to discover that plane of reality within him. Staring blankly at the floor, he watched Simone's reflection move as she did. Secluded enough in some random hall, no one seemed to hear her music and for that he was thankful. Philippe didn't know how to return to his father's labyrinth and he simply didn't want to. What would he say to him when he did? His ragged breathing made the card he clutched in his fist moisten.

Simone's music changed to short, cautious notes like a butterfly tripping over an unpredictable breeze. Concerned, for since her lack of speech he had learned to judge her through her music, he lifted his eyes, then his head to see her down the hall staring intently at her reflection in an ornate mirror. Rising, his legs went numb. Angry, wild notes as if that butterfly banged against a reflective chrysalis with no means of escape, poured out her violin next. Simone hadn't often seen her reflection and judging from her music, this time, she wasn't happy with what she saw.

That arrogant nobleman and his accursed reaction! The card crushed in his hand. *André Thaddus Marie, Vicomte de Chagny Faubourg St. Germain, Paris. Chagny! Always Chagny shifting and changing our lives like it now changes her music.*

Unable to bear the way she stood motionless as she played, eyes locked on her reflection, he hastened to her. Gently grabbing her shoulders, he turned her away from what she saw. The music she played spoke what his soul could not and he desperately needed her to be that extension of him. Dropping to one knee he brushed the air on either side of her face as if wiping away any invisible hurts that might change her music.

"Play, Angel. Play. None will look at you. I swear on my life. None will look on you that way again."

As if his words were a salve to an innocent soul, her foot began to tap, her hips sway and she played on, this time spinning around him like a thousand tops, carefree and happy. Philippe vowed to see to it her music always sounded that way and it would start by avenging his mother and making demands of Chagny.

He didn't know his way back to the labyrinth, but he could find the Faubourg St. Germain.

Chapter Thirteen

Paris from this height still looked the same. The wind whistled across the lead roof with a mournful moan while below the lights of a glamorous city twinkled gaily. Though he wanted to be charmed by that happy light, Vahid was dragged deeper into the clutches of the past. Someday he swore he would be either be free of Erik totally, or able to stand by his genius without study or fear. The rooftop door slammed shut behind him nearly bouncing Vahid off the moon.

The monster rose like a massive black bird near the base of Pegasus making Vahid question if the Phantom ever really left Paris. Erik moved too calmly. His utter control only meant that his mind rocked with something foreboding. There was no telling if he was studying the city or some manipulative plot in his mind. Panting from his winding climb up ladders and stairs, Vahid moved to the edge of the roof and surveyed Paris. It remained exquisite with the exception of that blasted new tower.

Genius perhaps, but what a god-awful eyesore.

"Why must you go to extremes, Erik?" His breath coated the air white. "If it's not the bowels of the earth, then it's practically the sky itself."

"Daroga, where have you been? I have been sitting here like a caged animal."

Vahid's side cramped. "Forgive me, your highness, for spending the better part of the day in Paris on your behalf." If he was able to see his face he was certain Erik glowered. "I delivered your blasted note. I wasn't about to let your son do it after all. The comte is ready to gather an army. If you wanted war—you have one. You are about to have all of Paris descend on you."

Erik leapt from his spot, his boots clanging loudly on the lead roof. The way that cloak of his spread added to the illusion of a bird. His massive form, dark clothing, and mask were countered only by the glow of his eyes. Poe's *Raven* slammed into Vahid's mind.

`Prophet!' said I, `thing of evil!—prophet still, if bird or devil!—Whether tempter sent, or whether tempest tossed thee here ashore...

"Where is Anna? I will not have the mother of my children kidnapped."

Often when Erik's voice held that throbbing control it was time to fear it. Vahid nearly swallowed his tongue in his efforts to force himself to speak. His lips made a popping sound as he pursed them. "Kidnapped you say? Interesting choice of words. Tell me, Erik, how does that feel?"

"Daroga, you are standing on a rooftop with a man who has a silk rope erotically caressing his right thigh. Do you really want to arouse me right now?"

"You are a fool. Do you have any idea what risk you are putting yourself in?"

"I came here to find my Anna. Now I implore you. Where is she?"

Vahid squinted hard as another line from Poe crept into his head.

Desolate yet all undaunted, on this desert land enchanted—On this home by horror haunted—tell me truly, I implore— "She is at the Chagny townhome—"

"You are blocking my path. Be a kind little man and step aside. I came here for Anna, nothing more."

Quoth the raven, `Nevermore'...

Vahid rubbed at his temple nervously, making his scrutiny of the lamplight below waiver. The monster trembled with some unarticulated frustration. He sensed it. It manifested in the slight twitches to Erik's hand. That letter made matters worse—far worse. He cursed himself for delivering it.

"Do you have any idea what risk you put your children in? You made the choice to put them first when you took them out of the security of that monastery. You can't run off half-crazed right now."

Erik touched his temple. He leaned in slightly. "I *am* half-crazed. What would you suggest I do?" With one graceful leap he pounced upon the railing and began to walk, stabbing the air with a finger. "My fuse is smoldering and every minute that passes without her is a minute of absolute agony. I am growing angry, Daroga."

"You're not in the position you used to be—"

"Daroga—"

"You go running out onto those streets right now after her and you are as good as dead!" Vahid uneasily eyed Erik's twitching hand. "There is not a shadow in this city that doesn't know the Phantom, regardless of this fair. You have children here to think of and clearly your state of mind can't handle a thing right now." His eyes shot from Erik's hand, to his mask and back to his hand. Erik balanced precariously on the edge of the rooftop. The wind snapped his cloak sending arrows of tension up Vahid's neck.

And the raven, never flitting, still is sitting, still is sitting, On the pallid bust of Pallas just above my chamber door; And his eyes have all the seeming of a demon's that is dreaming...

He swallowed hard. "You stay here. I will return to the comte and attempt to leave with Anna." Erik's eyes shifted abruptly, moved, and glowed at him from an even higher spot. Vahid spun, searching high and low for his evaporating specter. "I will Erik. When have I ever backed down on my word to you? You can't have the control when you are the one out of it. Don't do anything stupid. Do you hear me, Erik? Stay burrowed like the mole you are until I come to you to let you know all is clear. You have children to consider, you colossal fool!"

A disembodied voice filled with all the surge of a rising tide and floated menacingly around him.

"Get off my roof, Daroga."

* * * *

The organ bench splintered against the far wall. Turning from it, his hands convulsed upon the organ cabinet. He fought the urge to rip each stop out as if they were thorns imbedded in his side.

"Philippe? Simone! Where are you?"

Their names died as echoes. Where else to look? He left them only to collect his thoughts on the roof. Where could they have gone?

The world above moved at its precious pace while he remained deep below ground, burrowed like that mole. He spent hours searching the shadows only to come up empty.

Erik plucked at his temples again trying to deaden the noise in his mind. *Fail...fail...fail my Anna and now my children. I am a colossal fool. Never have I despised you, Dargoa, but I am being painted helpless when it is I who should be in control.*

Out of the corner of his eye, an ancient timepiece sat like a neglected, wicked thief. He picked up a brass paperweight.

Me! The Phantom of the Opera!

The brass paperweight shattered the clock's face, but not his tension.

Erik stared into his weak reflection in the fractured glass. Control lay elsewhere, in a confounded manhunt and an inescapable past. Somewhere several stories above, likely on the street alone and disoriented, were his children, while Chagny held Anna against her will.

The black-mask reflected a gloomy gray back at him. Erik curled his fingers to it until the edges bit mercilessly against his face. He felt his pulse in his fingertips.

I...should...stay...buried! In case they...return. Stay below ground and keep them safe. Yes... Yes... Erik should stay buried! No! Yes! Erik should have stayed buried from the very start! I curse you meddling in my life Philippe de Chagny. If not for you I would not have them. I would not need them! I would not feel human and would not have... Anna. Anna?

His body curled as if being burned alive. The noise in his head was all he could hear.

His life came full circle. He sat in solitude below an opera house planning his next move against Chagny. Yet when the image of their peaceful life in Germany tore his memories at the seams, Erik jerked his fingers off his mask, feeling his cold fingertips grow oddly warm with newly moving blood. He flexed his hands, then clenched them. It pumped more force behind his scream.

"Anna!"

Madness surged. It spread like a cancer. He went insane without her, slipping into personas he didn't want to revisit. His eyes rolled back, freeing him from his reflection and allowing him to give in to the noise in his mind. Air heaved in and out of his vacant nose. He had to end this ridiculous farce.

"By any means necessary!" His rage sent the already shattered clock careening down his drawing room stairs. He would end it if it killed him. End it for the sake of Philippe's gifts and Simone's precious outlook on the world. His children were now gone and his last scrap of sanity left with them.

"By any and all means!"

An intense calm washed over him with each heaving breath that filled his lungs. He no longer belonged in this realm. He was master of another and wouldn't remain buried like the dead. Not when he lived and could end this. He couldn't stay at his children's side without his children, and he was nothing to them without their mother.

The Daroga wouldn't return to the townhome and leave with Anna. He would.

The time had come. As a Phantom or man...the time had come.

* * * *

The Persian was wrong. He wasn't as good as dead. The streets of Paris had been oblivious to him. Erik was nothing more than a freak walking among freaks cloaked by the World's Fair. He prowled the streets, keeping to shadows nonetheless until he was ensconced in the Chagny townhome. It was just as ignorant as the Garnier had been years ago. Slipping in had been child's play. So much so, Erik thought perhaps he should have seeped into the hallowed halls of Chagny itself years ago and ended all this then. Better yet, he should have delivered his note himself and ripped the house down brick by brick until Chagny's presence in his life was nothing more than rubble and dust.

The two footmen stationed conspicuously outside a salon gave away Anna's location. A freak manipulation of his vocal chords was all it took for them to turn to the sweet voice coming from behind them. When they opened the doors to investigate, Erik stealthily followed. He pirouetted behind the open doors and out of sight. Watching with billowing impatience, the fools did a sloppy search for the disembodied intruder. They queried Anna. Her soft replies coursed blood through his veins. Convinced everything was normal and the sound was that of their weeping guest, the footmen left. Erik rounded from the door as soon as they shut it behind them. Spying her he felt the fragile veil between his sanity and madness lower slightly to cloak the demons in his mind.

"If I am dreaming, then do not let me wake. And if you are a ghost, then let me die right now."

"Erik?" Anna charged forward.

Catching her small frame mid leap, he crushed her to his chest. Lowering her to the ground only caused that veil to ripple and he pulled her back. From arm's length to his chest again, he battled with holding on and letting go. Sane or mad, he needed her and this charade had to end. How could he have become so complacent to their quiet life? How could he have let them steal her? He'd let his guard down. When he finally released her, despair turned to anger.

Her face...

"Who touched you?"

Anna glanced frantically to the door and pressed her fingers to his mouth. "Hush! Loup. The comte dismissed him. There is no telling where he is. There won't be much time before he turns on Chagny. We must get out of here."

Erik's eyes had clamped on the colors on her cheek. His hands shot forward. They roamed up and down her naked neck and raked through her short locks. "Your hair..." If he tried to twist her braid around his hands he would have been weaving air.

"What has this madness done to you?" He pawed at her shoulders, her waist, and up again searching for any sign of harm. "What else? What else has this done to you? This is all by Loup? *Loup*?" The meek nod and fresh tears in her eyes spoke volumes.

Panicked, Anna again pressed her hand to his mouth. "Erik, we will leave. Gather the children and simply flee. Where are they?"

The children? He looked down at her. *You innocent woman. It is for the children Erik will channel his anger and end all this once and for all.* His face contorted beneath his mask as if his words were a weapon and his body and mind the target. All emotion and regret left his voice. "Anna, do you still love me?"

"There was never a moment I didn't." She snatched his hands. "Come. Get us out of here. Let us go to the children and leave."

Erik didn't budge. This time it was he who gently pressed his finger to her lips. He stroked them as if caressing finely sculpted marble. "If you still love me, then you know it is too late to leave."

"Please, Erik, there is no time for this." She tugged his sleeve to try to get him to move.

"No, Anna. The noise will not go away. My fate is back. It is as if it is quivering, lurking, re-awakening and—" he looked to the window where beyond lay the dome of the Opera Garnier— "being played upon Apollo's Lyre."

His hand fluttered at her cheek. He attempted to brush the expression from her face. Erik kept his caress as light as he could so as not to hurt her further.

"I am so very, very angry, Anna. I am *Le Fantôme De L'Opéra.*" He stared into the emotion swimming in her eyes and his gaze went stone cold.

Anna tried to shush him silent by pressing her tear-coated kiss to his, but Erik wouldn't have it. Shaking her off was fruitless though. Her kiss sucked him out of the murk in his mind. He let her take over the control, then and there, since he knew soon she would have none. Anna's soft lips drugged him and for the brief moment he gave in to the high. He curled her deeply into the crook of his arm seeking shelter in her understanding and retreat in the powerful responses her body awakened in him.

Though he held her, it was Erik who clung to keep from falling.

Breaking their kiss, they listened to the silence that deadened the room.

"Where are our children, Erik? Phantom or not, I want to take you home."

The sound of her voice should have continued on as that drug that soothed his rotting mind, but instead, in breaking the kiss, he had said his good-bye.

"We are not going home. It is for their innocence. I can no longer allow my past to be an outworn history in our lives. It is a wound that continues to bleed. Anna, I love you more than music itself—and such is my soul. There is no melody to match the beauty you have brought me, but I end this now. My way."

"Where...where are they? Please? Erik?"

Her voice shook. His heart shook more.

"I don't know but I *will* find them, Anna. This *will* end."

He was sitting on the edge of so many things, the edge of fury, desire, danger, and ecstasy. As the silence increased and the concern he saw behind her eyes for her children grew greater, Erik closed his eyes and allowed himself to give into the noise releasing him to fall over the edge and not just one of them, but all of them...

Chapter Fourteen

The muscles of his cheek jumped as Philippe clenched his jaw tighter.

He wasn't a lying beggared and the servant accusing him of such was in danger of having his teeth knocked out if he didn't permit them at least through the threshold. Simone shivered against his leg as chilly blasts of air knifed them in the back. He was thankful he had the presence of mind to keep his sister's hood up and her face tipped to the floor, thus sparing the Chagny townhome a horrific awakening, but he was thinking better of it now. Perhaps scaring the daylights out of the insufferable footman would get him to move faster.

Philippe shoved the vicomte's card hard against the man's chest

"Did you not hear me correctly the first two times? My name is Philippe Georges Marie."

His eyes bored blood draining holes into the servant's back when he finally left, card in gloved hand. Though left waiting only a few minutes it seemed like hours before the man returned and escorted them to the drawing room. The comtess and vicomte would attend them soon.

The tension in his jaw threatened to overtake his entire body. Massaging his eyes until he saw stars, Philippe paced the richly appointed room trying hard not to study the fantastic and ornate trimmings he saw through the tiny stars now dancing in his vision. Red and blue hues stirred to life giving the room an inviting air.

Nothing of this is inviting. Nothing, nothing, nothing. Mein Gott, Simone...

He huffed in annoyance and blew air out his nose. Stilling Simone's hands for a fourth time as he passed her, he forced her to lower the violin and bow from her chin.

Whatever you want to say right now, it can wait. I don't want to hear it.

The rings he saw rimming her eyes nearly forced his fist through the closest wall more than once. Instead, his pressed his palms against a waist high table and breathed deeply. The aroma of roses filled his nose but didn't calm him. Out of the corner of his eye he saw Simone inch her violin under her chin again.

I want out of this. I just want my mother, my father back to normal, Simone not to be disturbed and Chagny to go away forever.

His chin sagged to his chest. She was softly tapping the bow to the strings now like a child dancing with a need to relieve herself. He rolled his head to face her and nodded. Who was he to stop her?

Let her play and rattle the bones in the catacombs for all I care. This entire situation is such a mess it might as well be set to music.

* * * *

"You test me in extraordinary means, Daroga."

The tip of his walking stick clicked off his impatience as Raoul attempted to finish a mind-clearing walk. There was a chill to the air and it made him pick up his pace the closer he got to his townhome. The Persian, spry for his old age, kept up. Erik's note, damp from the mist, crumbled as Raoul rammed it into his waistcoat pocket.

"Rightful you should shove that away finally," the Persian said. "Staring at it will do nothing to change the fact that history is repeating."

"Did you return here merely to state the obvious, Daroga?"

"I returned to knock sense into you. The only rational thing you've done is dismiss that lack-wit bounty hunter. You speak now of running off to the Opera Garnier in search of Erik? You are a gentleman, not an investigator! I've sent you to opera houses across the world for legitimate reasons, but think of it. A criminal never returns to the scene of his crimes. It's madness. I already searched the Opera house. I told you. It remains as it was. To go there now is wasted time. Prudence is the way to answers, Monsieur. Your answers lie with

Mademoiselle Barret. Remain safe in your house and find what you can from her. Let professionals deal with tracking Erik."

Raoul stopped mid jog up the broad steps of his residence. "You don't understand that I simply don't trust you, do you Daroga? I don't trust anyone any longer." He tapped him dead center of his chest with the tip of his stick. "For years you sat on the outskirts of everything and now you are more than willing to offer advice and help? I don't trust anyone to take care of anything relating to the Phantom but me." The door opened as if on cue. Raoul marched inside, the Daroga in his wake. He spoke as his staff relieved him of his coat and hat. "Your constant badgering to release the girl to your custody only raises my suspicions over your involvement."

His tension wound higher when he spied Christine and André at the far end of the hall moving as if part of a funeral march. Legard hastened his way forward ahead of them.

Raoul slid his waistcoat aside, put a hand on his hip. He flicked the footman away. "What is it, Legard? Everyone seems under a blasted dark cloud and I don't mean the one that has been following me." He jerked his head toward the Persian. His wife and son paused outside the distant doors to the drawing room. André had slid a hand to her shoulder. "Is it Christine?" Raoul lowered his voice. "André?"

"Quite the opposite. While you were gone a most unprecedented guest arrived to call on Chagny. The staff alerted me immediately. We were about pay a visit to the drawing room."

Something was off. He knew Legard. The man was as straightforward as an arrow. "Judging from your lack of panic I assume it is not the Phantom."

Christine's face appeared paler the closer he got.

"No. It is Philippe Georges Marie."

Raoul stopped short. The Persian nearly slammed into his back.

"I find no humor in that, Legard."

"Neither do I," the Daroga echoed cautiously.

Raoul schooled his features and addressed Christine and his son. "Whatever the meaning of this is, I want both of you to pay it no mind. I'll not have one thing upsetting either of you."

His hand stopped on the doorknob. The air around them hummed with a sweet and strange music. Raoul warned everyone with one glance before he shoved open the door.

What in all of Heaven...

A gasp leapt from Christine's mouth. Raoul pulled her protectively back against him.

A small child, back to them, stood on his ottoman in the center of the room. The youth to her side pushed off the side table and snapped to attention. He bowed respectfully. Lifting his hand he bade the girl to be silent in an elegant move that could have come from the most accomplished Maestro. The little girl didn't turn around. She merely lowered her violin and laid her head upon the young man's shoulder. She stared out the window.

"What is the meaning of this?" Raoul insisted as Legard and the Persian pushed forward behind him. He released Christine to Legard. "You have some nerve to enter this home young man and disrespect the name of a respected Frenchman. Whoever you are I suggest you start speaking and speaking the truth, for I will not have Chagny treated in such an egregious manner."

"What disrespect, Monsieur? I enter this home by invitation of your Vicomte."

"My Vicomte?" Raoul shot a look at André who sagged to one leg, his regard suddenly on the floor. When he looked up, Raoul noted the turmoil behind his eyes.

"I am Philippe Georges Marie and lies are pointless. They only breed scandal and I tend to dislike scandal."

That phrased smacked Raoul across the face like a challenger's glove. The boy sounded exactly like the note's author.

"I won't be played with like a mouse, Monsieur," Raoul warned. "Give me your entire name before I have you arrested and escorted out of here."

"I lack a surname and we're not going anywhere until questions about our mother's whereabouts are answered."

"Mother?" The little girl hopped off the ottoman and turned.

Nothing prepared him. Nothing...

Raoul's heart raced as if he ran for miles. Shock rose on Christine's face as it dripped of color. Her dainty hands trembled like a fall leaf. Legard had slammed his eyes shut and turned away, his thumb and forefinger pinching the bridge of his nose. André averted as well, gripping his mother's arm and staring at the floor. Acid crept from Raoul's stomach to his throat. There was no tearing his eyes away from the abomination before him. The little girl stared up at him, her softly bizarre yellow eyes studying him as openly as he did her. She cocked her head curiously and hugged the violin. The innocent expression skewed her face into a macabre oxymoron. Instinctually, Raoul positioned himself between his wife and son. The Persian didn't flinch.

"You move as though we are a threat, Monsieur le Comte." Philippe draped his hand across the girl's shoulders. "Simone is merely a child and I would thank you not to look on her as if she were a monster."

Raoul filled his burning lungs and let the air seep out tightly clenched teeth. He never dreamed he would grind out his next words. "Where is your father?"

"Where my father is, is not the question. The question regards our mother. Did you take her? She did nothing to warrant such. Isn't that right, Comtess?"

Like a match to a powder keg, chain reactions exploded around the room. Christine's stammers bounced down Raoul's spine while André's fervor for respect of his mother resulted in Raoul holding him back with a quick block of his arm.

"Enough!" Raoul commanded. "Your father is solely responsible for this outrage and I'll have you confirm for me, *right now*, his whereabouts. I assure you no harm or blame will come to you or that girl."

"*That* girl? Her name is Simone! You dare blame my family for this ridiculous manhunt when the entire thing could end with one confession from your wife?"

Raoul forced his hand harder against the thoroughbred that had replaced his son.

"You will treat the Comtess de Chagny with the respect she is due young man—" Legard interjected.

"A liar begets no respect, Monsieur le Comte," Philippe spat. "My parents saved her life. She is well aware. Inquire such of the Daroga. He told me all."

Raoul's nostrils flared. He took two strides toward Philippe. "You will leave the Comtess de Chagny out of this and tell me his whereabouts immediately. Chagny will not be threatened by him or disrespected by you—"

"My father is not a threat to anyone. He is—"

"A murderer and a manipulative madman!"

The air erupted with intense music. It cut down Raoul's words as if they were a saber through butter. An agonizing tune arched wildly, Simone's music filling the room as if a thousand voices screamed in unison. Crazy-eyed, she leaned against her strings, her fingers flying faster with each passing second.

"Simone," Philippe cried, but she wouldn't respond. "Simone!"

She backed herself farther toward a corner.

"For the love of God, make her stop," Raoul shouted, his ears ringing painfully.

Christine clutched her temples. "What possesses her? Raoul! Legard! Daroga!"

"Dear Lord, is she mad?" Legard rubbed viciously at his earlobe.

"She is not mad," Philippe yelled over the din. "The violin is her voice! You have made her cry! All of you and your prejudices and manhunts! You did this to her! *You have hurt my sister!*" Swinging his back to them he knelt before her, ducking her bowing arm several times before he managed to seize it. The music screeched to a violent halt. "It's alright, Angel," he cooed. "Calm down. I'm here. They won't hurt you. I promised you, didn't I? No one will ever hurt my Angel of Music, no one."

Angel of Music? Raoul jerked his fingers off his ears. That phrase set the past into the present with a blinding intensity. The note in Raoul's pocket practically burned a hole into his chest.

"If Erik is anywhere," he replied sharply, "he is at that opera house." Raoul marched toward the boy and shoved the note into Philippe's hands. A powerful current coursed between them. "I should have acted on my instinct far sooner and ignored the suggestions of the Persian. Your father is what I say, Monsieur. And we end this now. Angels of Music do not exist. Madmen do."

Chapter Fifteen

"Are you so certain of that, Monsieur?" The words leveled the room like an earthquake before it faded into mind-numbing silence. Erik left Anna in the doorway and crossed the room, circling Raoul and his shocked children once before turning. Only Christine's voice lifted the lid of the coffin-like stillness.

"My God. Erik..."

He had tried not to look at her, more captivated by the ending strains of Simone's music which had led him from the salon to her side, but now he had no choice. Instantly, air drained from his lungs. Seeing Christine's face and hearing her voice, once the sweet drug of years past, now served to mix his decisions. He closed his eyes, studying the afterglow of her image in the darkness.

He opened them, and with a determined stare looked at Legard, the Persian, and an extraordinary youth to her side.

"Monsieur le Vicomte, I presume?"

The boy didn't have to reply. He looked strikingly like his father. Christine inched toward Raoul and leaned into him.

Still inwardly afraid and uncertain of the Angel of Music after all these years? It matters not. The past will soon be over.

Erik looked on his children as he walked around the center of the room. Circling wouldn't settle his thoughts. Acting on them would. "It has been awhile, Monsieur le Comte. Have you nothing to say?"

"I will say everything I need when they cast your sentence."

Impressive. The boy has a backbone after all these years. Erik stopped circling.

"Have your say before I have you arrested," Raoul threatened.

"My sentence you say?"

He chuckled seconds before moving. He hooked Raoul's neck with one arm, cutting off his command for Legard to stand by Christine. Erik twisted Raoul's arms behind his back.

"Stand down, Monsieur Legard, and reach for that pistol not a second more. I will have my say or I will end this in a manner I wish *not!*" Legard spread his arms and nodded. The Persian had the presence of mind to move closer to Philippe and Simone. Erik turned his attention back to the man bucking in his arms.

"*My sentence,*" he roared, "has already been cast!" Releasing one hand, Erik tore off his mask and shoved it against Raoul's face. "Look through it. Is it tight? Hot? Do you feel that biting along its edge?" Erik pressed it harder against his face. "Do you see that outline around the eyes? It is always there, it never goes away." Erik wrenched his arms tighter. Raoul rose to the tips of his toes and grunted. "When I take this mask off your face however, *you* have instant freedom."

Erik shoved Raoul aside, freeing him from his arms and the black-masked prison. The comte staggered before looking up, then away.

"See what I mean?" Erik snarled. "All these years and you still cannot look at me. I can remove the mask, but the face is still there and you have made it so no matter where I go, the two cannot be separate. Because of you no matter where *we* went, the past was there to greet us."

"Are you trying to play the victim, Erik?" Raoul lifted his chin like a battle ready rebel.

"The victims are my children."

"What?"

"My son,"—he nodded toward him—"Philippe Georges Marie, was born in an abandoned barn somewhere between here and Germany. I laid Anna down on a filthy horse blanket out of the way of the leaking roof and vermin, and delivered him myself because there was no midwife around who did not know my face."

"What does that have to do with a life of lies and murder? You orchestrated your despicable destiny, not I."

"My daughter," Erik continued loudly, "was born in a small village she dearly misses. She feels safe there, but because of how this manhunt has made the world fear this,"—he pointed roughly to his face—"and how you have made certain *my* past is attached to it, my little girl lives in fear of the day she will receive her mask." He replaced his somberly. "I can see it in her eyes. She has been condemned enough. I will not have children a part of this any longer. They are too young to spend their lives looking over their shoulders because of a past they did not create. I cannot give Christine what she needs to end this insanity, but I can give you want you want."

"What is it Christine wants?"

Erik followed his gaze to her. "Could you be married to her all these years and not know?"

"I am fully aware of the command you still have over her."

"My power over her was severed years ago. It is the command she has over you that you refuse to see. My question is what is this doing to your son? If she can't completely love you, does she completely love him?"

"You bastard!"

Raoul's fist cracked across Erik's jaw. His face shot to the side as he took that punch and suppressed ever fiber to react.

"What is it you're doing, Erik?"

Erik rubbed his jaw. Noise rang perversely in his ears. "Ending this. I am through with giving in to a madman! I lived in solitude thinking this was behind us. I had finally been rewarded with some small scrap of normalcy. However, so long as memories are perpetuated my family will never be free. Ending it cannot come on your end, because if it could this would have been over years ago. So I end it now. Do what you want with me; just leave my family in peace."

"Peace? The Phantom talks of peace?" Raoul almost laughed. "How do I know those are not just some valiant words you are throwing me before you strike me down right here?"

"If I had ever wanted to kill you I would have done it a thousand times over already, but I promised your brother."

Raoul flinched.

"You will never live up to the man he was, so cringe when I mention him all you want," Erik said. "Make your choice. Either you trust the years where you *never* saw my face, or you do not and you cut me down. Let me rot in a prison for all it will spare the family I secretly desired. I suggest you act now.

You are trying my patience and I am losing my will for control."

"He tries *your* patience? How bloody quaint."

Anna's shriek stopped them in their tracks as Loup's words and laugh filled the room. All eyes shot to the door.

"Correct, Messures, I am right behind *mon alouette* like I have been her entire life. What did you expect? I would slink away without taking her, without getting anything out of this for myself?" Loup moved into the room, a pistol appearing as if from thin air. He pressed it tightly to Anna's forehead.

Blind and malevolent hatred flared within Erik. As soon as he lunged forward, the pistol was twisted and Anna's cry rang in his ears.

"One move," Loup shouted. "Make one more move and I swear I will level your pretty little Anna before your eyes. A bullet can be triggered faster than a Phantom, Monsieur. Don't tempt me, any of you."

He sucked Anna's earlobe into his mouth making her shake from tip to toe. It made a popping sound when he released it. Erik's fury grew.

"Forgive me for interrupting your casual conversation." Loup was smug. "Now with all of you under my gun, I have all I need to control this charade. While it's been fun playing games with Chagny over who would pay me more for the Phantom—the comte or comtess—oh please, now is not the time to look so baffled, Monsieur le Comte. She came running the instant you dismissed me. Promised me double what you pay to keep Erik *out* of your reach. This, in addition to the money she's been paying me to keep her love for the monster a secret from you, how could I refuse?"

Christine's breath hitched as her face invented a new shade of white. Erik glanced from her to Raoul noting his lips disappear beneath his moustache.

"You lying, manipulative bastard." Raoul's voice was deadly.

"Believe what you will. Having the Phantom show up here would take the opportunity from me and we can't have that now, can we? You all think to arrogantly end this affair when it is *my* turn for the glory?" A wicked laugh filled the room. "You have denied me for the last time Monsieur le Comte and are officially in *my* way."

Keeping Anna's head locked in the jaws of his arm, Loup swung the pistol directly at Raoul's face. Christine screamed, flinging herself against her husband. Raoul whirled her away, their bodies twisting to the floor.

"You madman!" Raoul shouted.

Loup aimed low. "If she is thinking to shield you, it is of no matter. A bullet can pass through two. Now pay me what you owe me! Remember, a bullet flies fast and straight and only I know the target. Either I get money or someone will die."

The pistol trigger cocked igniting enough murder in Erik for a legion of men. Widespread panic flooded the room. His rage rang loud as he went toward Loup. Christine's scream rent the air. Anna's cry stabbed his heart. Raoul cursed at him, and Erik barely heard his yell for Legard to shoot.

Panic filled the air. The small crowd dispersed in a confused mass as the women screamed and a child yelled at her father.

Two shots crossed in the air.

And the world stopped spinning.

Chapter Sixteen

The aroma of gunpowder was replaced by metallic tendrils of blood. A superhuman cry of rage clawed its way out of Erik's throat. He flew past Legard, forcing him to twirl his body to the side as Erik dove for Loup. Erik caught him mid escape.

In seconds, a blood stopping crunch ripped the air as Erik's grief wrenched the bones apart in Loup's neck. Huffing heavily, Erik's hands sprung open. The bounty hunter dropped to the floor with a lifeless thud and silence stood so deep even the human heart questioned its right to beat.

Anna backed off, swimming with her arms and legs away from where she was thrown, and away from the twisted body of Loup. She rolled and crawled hand over hand toward the other body on the floor. Erik staggered as well to the motionless bundle that lay silently between him, Anna, Raoul, and Christine.

"Simone? Si...Simone?" He sank to the floor—first one knee, then the next. "Simone?"

Tiny ringlets fanned across her face. Beside her feet, her beloved violin and bow lay silent. Her eyes were closed, her breathing barely there. He stroked the hair from her face, terrified at the crimson spreading across her dress and down one tiny arm. He rocked, back and forth and back again, his hands not knowing what to touch or where to go. He was choked by the presence of the Reaper over his shoulder. He pressed his palm against her blood.

When he screamed, Paris recoiled.

Erik dragged himself to his feet and stumbled drunkenly toward Raoul. "My little girl! Why? Erik's little girl!"

Christine gripped Raoul until she was white knuckled. Anna's whimpers jerked Erik's head back to his family. She clung glassy eyed and open mouthed to Philippe's pant leg.

Erik staggered and struggled to lift Simone into his arms. His hands shook violently.

Winded, Legard pushed his way forward. "Give her to me. Let me have her. Monsieur, please. *You must release her to me!*"

Erik shook his head in a confused daze as Legard pried her out of his desperate grip. Simone's head fell lax against his shoulder. Legard slowly backed away stopping only when Raoul's hand shot up and grabbed the hem of his waistcoat.

"Whatever it takes, Jules. Use whatever I have. Drain my accounts, sell Chagny, *sell my soul*! Whatever it takes, do not return and tell me that little girl has died..."

It is to the credit of human nature, that, except where its selfishness is brought into play, it loves more readily than it hates. Hatred, by a gradual and quiet process, will even be transformed to love, unless the change be impeded by a continually new irritation of the original feeling of hostility.— Nathaniel Hawthorne, *The Scarlet Letter*

Chapter Seventeen

Nothing was deeper or darker than the grief found in questioning the outcome of the unknown. Try as one may to control the unpredictable, the only partner to grief was time. Sometimes it healed. Other times, like now, time stood as a faceless, nameless presence that couldn't be turned back. Like a curious pilgrim, perpetual queries searched his mind for answers he didn't possess until his thoughts had him twisted around so well he hardly recognized himself.

"He was turning himself over to me, Christine," Raoul muttered. She stood at his side but he kept his forearms upon his thighs and his eyes on his boots. "And a child pays the price."

Christine didn't reply. Part of him didn't want her to. Not with the questions dragging through his mind. The door at the far end of the hall opened. Collectively the group gathered in the small waiting area of a Paris hospital sucked in breath—but Raoul released his in a slow, steady stream. He tapped his son's thigh as he stood. André sat stoically next to him, his head hung low between his arms. At the far window, Erik stood, back to them all, Legard and his Inspectors cautiously close behind. Anna was curled in a chair, near catatonic in her stares as her son and the Persian stood vigil.

It was Raoul's manhunt that brought them here and he felt the weight of that crush his shoulders and burn behind his eyes.

"It is difficult," the doctor explained. "She hasn't regained consciousness yet from the surgery. I would be lying if I didn't mention the possibility that she never will. Not a child that young."

"*Oh, dear God,*" Christine whispered.

"You can't come out here and tell us that!" Philippe's outburst ripped the hall in two and jerked Raoul's attention his way. "You have to fix this! I can't be without my sister!"

The boy rounded his hand into a fist. Before it could collide with bone crushing force to the wall, Raoul lurched. His hand landed like a rock on Philippe's shoulder forcing him firmly, but carefully, to a seat.

"Is it possible for a heart to change rhythm?"

Raoul looked up as Erik's voice floated woefully from the window. He spent the last few hours staring at Paris as if contemplating the world's ultimate betrayal against him. Night deepened, making the only thing staring back into the room being the reflection of his yellow eyes. Ordinarily it would have chilled Raoul incomparably, but instead he saw in them that same searching pilgrim.

"A heart can love, wilt, hate, but can it change the way it beats?" Erik turned.

Raoul swore he saw unshed tears glistening behind those very human eyes. It could have unmanned him.

"Is it possible for love to truly be like music? So flawless in its beauty that if you displace one note the entire piece diminishes? So strong that a father would rather die than see his children suffer? Somebody tell me. I never truly had a father's love. I never heard such music."

André had looked up. Raoul met Erik's eyes and shared a tormented gaze. His hand tightened into Philippe's shoulder. Erik eyed Anna intently.

"When Simone was born, I knew what I had passed to her and I wanted to die. I wanted *her* to die with me. Does such make me a bad father?" Erik leveled his eyes on Raoul. "Because I took it back. I repented. I took it back."

Raoul for once had no desire to shy away from the intensity of Erik's gaze. He tried to stammer a reply, but what answers did he have? Erik turned to Anna again.

"Her eyes never reflected anything but the wonder of a child. Anna?" Erik choked. "I need her back."

Raoul's soul withered. He remembered the agony of his own daughter's death as if it were as fresh as the coming dawn.

"I need my little girl," Erik begged. "There is something in her that is different. I cannot hear the music without her. My son cannot mature without her. They complete each other." He glanced at Philippe curling his arms as if trying to hug bare air. "I cannot *feel* anything. Someone make me feel *something*, because feeling nothing hurts."

Raoul heard himself swallow and wondered if the rest did. In the years he shared his life entwined with Erik's, he never once saw a man behind the monster. Anna stood. She reached up with a quivering hand and removed Erik's mask. Raoul swallowed again. For the first time he could recall, that savage face didn't repulse him, but held him transfixed. He didn't trust the feeling. She dried the tears on Erik's savaged cheeks as he looked down at her. Standing there, Raoul felt like an intruder.

"I see her in you. How will I be able to keep on if I see her in you?" Erik whispered.

"I know, Erik." She wiped a tear from his golden eye. "I see her in you too."

"She has to grow up, so she can tell you our secret. She promised me she would tell you what it is like. *She promised.*"

"What secret? What promise?"

Erik rested his forehead against hers. He intimately grabbed the back of her neck. "She promised she would tell you what it is like for a daughter to be adored by her father, for a daughter to be so completely and utterly loved by her father."

Raoul cursed. He dropped Christine's hand and slid his other off Philippe's shoulder. Anna's tears shook her body. She collapsed into Erik's arms.

It's the children who always show the mature the stark reality of their mistakes.

"Go. She needs you to sing to her." Anna gently pushed him toward the room. All watched as Erik slipped away and silently shut the door behind him.

"Mademoiselle Barret," Raoul whispered. "I cannot find the words to say how sorry I am for—"

"Not now, Monsieur le Comte. Let my family listen to his Abendlied."

Chapter Eighteen

Simone should be outside, playing for the chickens and spinning like a fool in mad circles. Free from the confines of anything but her spirit. Instead, beds flanked her. They ran the length of both sides of the room. Some were protected by fabric partitions, but not hers.

Arms folded, weight distributed evenly on both feet and his chest out, Philippe hovered over her bedside. A dull ache wound behind his lower back. He could move, but refused. Standing like a fortress made him feel impenetrable. It took all his effort to tear his mother away from Simone's side so she could return to the Persian's care. Hours had passed and his father was nowhere to be found.

A nun shuffled by. He nodded politely and waited until she was gone to dig his thumb and forefinger against his eyes. He tried to pluck the sleep from them, or at least the image of Simone getting shot from his memory.

"Monsieur?"

He drew his hand down his face. Philippe's fingers stopped at his chin before he lifted it to the ceiling. His hand turned to a rock-hard fist. He scrubbed his mouth with the back of it.

"Monsieur le Vicomte." He cleared his throat.

"I told you. I go against convention. You may call me André."

"You hardly acted against convention when I came calling yesterday, Monsieur."

"That was yesterday." He laid something on the foot of the bed. "Your sister's violin. I hope you don't mind that I have it and I procured a case."

Philippe eyes narrowed. Was that some sort of peace offering? He had to force his fist not to return to his mouth. The violin seemed to be dying too.

"Even a stranger could see your sister was...is...attached to it. Can I get you anything? Perhaps you are hungry, or in need of a drink?" He gestured down the ward. "I can take you anywhere you want—"

"I'm not leaving this bedside."

"Has there been any change?"

What do you care? Philippe widened his legs. "None. The doctors come and go but there's no change. If I could, I would remove her from this abysmal place entirely. Take her someplace else to rest and heal and hold her until—" Philippe looked away, feeling his helplessness. He snapped his head back to André. "Why are you here, Monsieur? Our families are at war."

André didn't remove his eyes from Simone's face. Its pallor made it more skull-like, but the nobleman didn't react like before. Hours ago he wanted to charge Philippe down like an angry bull. Now he stared in compassion upon Simone.

Philippe didn't trust it.

"That may be true," André replied. "Though I may be my father's son, does that make me like him? You certainly are different from yours."

Grinding his teeth made Philippe's jaw tighten again. "You need not be cordial to me in light of my sister. I know I am the son of the Phantom."

"Right now, you are a man standing vigil over his sister's bedside. A noble and honorable act. Can we lose the pretenses and allow that to be the case?"

Philippe looked at him warily out of the corner of his eye.

"If you are anything like me," André continued carefully, "then your life has been an intricate web of half-truths. I don't pretend to know all the details that brought us to this egregious outcome. Only that *my* parents were hunting *yours* and you are the namesake of a man I adore, but never met. My *parents* perpetrated this. Not *me*. I thank you for not judging me by their tangled obsessions."

His words heavily forced Philippe to the stool beside the bed. It thumped back on two legs sending a boom throughout the ward. The place soon was as silent as before. He pressed his forearm to his thigh as he stared at the violin. "Thank you for retrieving that."

Philippe looked up long enough to see André nod as he studied the shallow rise and fall of Simone's chest.

"This was not supposed to happen," he quietly mused. "I don't think any of this was supposed to happen." Philippe chewed his sarcasm.

"What do you understand of it...Philippe?"

Philippe stared at his sister, his brows knitting a history he didn't create. For once in his life there was someone sitting across from him who was an equal of sorts. He never could live up to the genius of his father, nor understand the sensitive mind behind the madman. He was too brilliant himself to be one with vagabonds, and too exuberant to be satisfied with monks. Though he and André were as different as fox and hound, they had matured in the same chase. What *did* he understand of it?

He took the imaginary olive branch. "Nothing, frankly. Nothing beyond I am Philippe Georges Marie, and this is my sister." His arm was heavy when he indicated Simone. "I lived my life trying to understand the past that tangles my name to yours, but I lived it being loved by the man your family so hates. The man who loves us in the way he knows how, and who loves my mother more than life. That much I understand. That's worth something in all this."

"You speak highly of love, then. My father worships my mother, but she..." André's voice dipped and with it his eyes. "Do you understand him, your father? I often don't mine."

"Sometimes. It's the world that doesn't understand him, and sadly they may now never understand Simone." He reached for the violin case and removed the instrument. He reverently tucked it to her chest and wrapped her frail arms around it.

"I don't think my parents understand." André was somber. "But I would, if you enlighten me."

Philippe looked up. André's fingertips rested on the bed as if he desired to touch a flaxen curl and comfort Simone, but the past was still too raw for such a tentative display of friendship. Philippe stroked the hair out of her face.

"André, to understand them, is to understand music..."

* * * *

137

Her hand slid dejectedly down a fabric partition two beds away. Christine gripped the partition's edge to steady herself as she listened to a tale of The Angel of Music she'd never heard before. Years of grief flowed silently down her face as Philippe told about Erik, and in turn, Anna. He unraveled a story of their life beyond the uncertainty of a manhunt. One built on a love she longed to own, but didn't possess.

As long as she breathed she would never forget André's uncompleted sentence: *My father worships my mother, but she...*

She shut your father out pursuing a love that was never as true as his. Christine's silent confession soaked her chin in tears.

Hearing her son ask careful questions, listening to Philippe ask his own in reply, painted a picture of what time had done to the young lives that never asked to be shaped in such a way. Christine backed away knowing in that moment she could never have Erik and would never love the same again. His soul belonged to another, and it was not Anna.

It belonged to Simone.

It wasn't that which sent her racing out of the ward. Her soul belonged to another as well and she prayed that it wasn't too late for love to be made whole.

* * * *

The patterns he paced through the long corridor were to be cathartic. Nothing helped. He linked his fingers together behind his back squeezed them hard, just to feel *something.* Raoul kept seeing the bullet tear through Simone as she plummeted to the floor like a flightless bird. He pivoted in the same spot as two minutes ago and switched directions. The image gave chase.

Never did I think I would ever sympathize with a madman. He stopped wringing his hands and slid aside his waistcoat. He shook his head and looked out the window. *Traitorous reflection! It is more composed than I am. I know nothing of Erik beyond the monster he is. But now I see him as a father and, God help me, the two images are rioting within me.*

Raoul lifted a hand and slowly slid it through his hair. He massaged the back of his head. His heart leaked agony as his arms remembered holding his daughter's lifeless body. He would never wish it on a living soul—not even Erik.

"Raoul?"

He closed his eyes to the lilt of his wife's voice. "Christine."

"There has been no change with her."

"I'm aware and responsible."

"You are not responsible, Raoul. I am."

"Christine—"

"No, Raoul. It is time I spoke."

Only on stage did Christine's voice find such passion, but this was no opera. Something foreboding pinched his eyes as his wife fluttered like a lost butterfly.

"How can I possibly make you understand? I yearned for his guidance and became seduced with the *illusion* of the Angel of Music. Then I realized he was nothing more than a man."

He warily tipped his head. "I know all this, Christine."

"You know nothing of it! I rejected *a man* and his gifts due to my own foolish immaturity."

"Christine?" Raoul took her by the shoulders. "You rejected a manipulative *madman*. You only assumed you loved and sympathized with him as a defensive way to protect yourself. Why are you dredging up the past? Merely because of the emotion he displayed? Simply because he has children does not eliminate what he put you through. I sympathize with him as well now. I lost a daughter I love. I'm torn inside because I identify with him in this. I long to make amends to that little girl, but I can't let go of what he did to you. Not now, not ever."

"He is mad because of me!"

"Christine. You are not responsible for that man's madness."

"In truth, I am responsible for much, because of how deeply I foolishly love him."

"You...what?"

"Loup spoke the truth. I love him. I always have."

Raoul's hands found his hips, this time to form a block against the absurdity of her confession. But it wasn't absurd. He knew...it leached out the way she paced. It screamed in her voice. Her confession was a rotated puzzle piece suddenly clicking into place. Raoul fought the tension in his jaw to allow her to speak, for if he opened his mouth right now he wasn't sure what would pass his lips.

"I was his first love, Raoul, but he was not mine. The boy who rescued my scarf was. I love you with all my heart. My selfish, wretched jealousy perpetuated this entire manhunt. I never confessed years ago because so long as you vowed to protect me from Erik it meant you were looking for him, and there was still a chance for me to experience his love."

"Confessed what?"

What he heard next over the course of Christine's halted and awkward admissions, from Erik saving her life from Richard Barret, to the blackmail by Loup and the new arrangement she made with him, turned his world upside down.

"All these years I have wanted you both," Christine wailed, tearfully. "I've been a jealous fool! A selfish fool! I still have my child and he may very well lose his, and dear God when I think of losing my family! Teach me how to love my family the *right* way. In the way he has come to love Anna and his son, and his...dear God, Raoul, she is only a little girl! *What have I done?*"

Christine collapsed into his arms, sobbing with her entire body. Dumbstruck, Raoul had to force his arms to curl around her. Looking around, he searched for his sanity. Instead a pair of yellow eyes hovered in the window's reflection. Raoul's spine stiffened. The eyes grew larger as Erik stepped forward, his gnarled, outstretched hand appearing in the glassy surface. Was he reaching for Raoul's neck or Christine's shoulder? When he looked behind him the only thing he glimpsed was Erik's cape as he disappeared around the corner.

Chapter Nineteen

Bright morning sun bathed the Tuileries. The garden was alive with couples on lover's strolls. The city of lights loved as usual while Erik's heart beat wooden in his chest. Row after row of roses burst into full bloom sending their heady fragrance floating through the morning air. Erik caressed them lightly as he roamed, aimlessly pausing every now and then to select the most perfect, unblemished ones he could. Last time he wandered this garden he kept to shadows like a demented stalker. He cared less now who looked on him or how this manhunt ultimately ended. The only care he had in the world lay in a bed that swallowed her whole. He gently reached to a rose. Its red petals folded in on one another, not totally asleep, yet not totally awake, much like Simone. Erik snapped the stem. Dew splattered against his wrist. He lifted the rose to the false nose on his mask.

"The Persian suspected you might be here, if not in the opera house."

That voice shredded his brain. The great and noble Raoul came seeking him, instead of hunting him? Erik lifted his eyes from the delicate flower and pinned them on the comte. Raoul waved off the police that accompanied him and strode forward. So he wouldn't shrink in the presence of the Phantom any longer? Erik addressed the rose.

"It takes my daughter's blood for you to call off your hounds?"

"The escort is Legard's doing. You're not exactly in your right mind, leaving your child and coming out in public like this."

The folds of the rose were soft beneath Erik's fingers. Should he remove the thorns or would it be best for Simone to know that things of beauty often come with their ugly side as well? "I don't care about the public and why would I not be in

141

my right mind, Monsieur?" *Leave the_thorns.* Erik walked the hedgerow ignoring Raoul's footfalls behind him.

"There are people worried about you. You should return to the hospital."

"No, it is not time. When she wakes she will need a bouquet, a perfect one, for a perfect little girl." He scrutinized another rose ignoring the long cast of Raoul's shadow as it fell in front of him.

"You say when she awakens, but—"

Erik raised his hand and cut him off. A white rose perhaps? *No, the yellow ones to match her eyes.* "Who tends these gardens?"

"I've no idea."

"They need to plant more yellow." Erik trained his own yellow eyes on his nemesis. "So a thousand golden eyes can stare at you every time you come out here. Why *did* you come looking for me? Could not the Persian? Or do you suddenly feel guilty and this act is some noble gesture to make you feel useful? Or perchance you come here to kill me lest your wife's confession in that hallway suddenly turn my heart over to her? I assure you, Monsieur, the games between she and I ended long ago."

Raoul shifted, glanced to the police, and shifted again. His little box step betrayed his nerves.

"You need to return. Mademoiselle Barret is asking for you, as is your son. I've a carriage waiting." He gestured to Erik's clothing. "The Persian sent a fresh shirt."

The crimson color of Simone's blood had faded to a murky brown. He pawed at it, rubbing it against his chest as if trying to get her blood to flow directly into his heart. "No. I need a part of her close."

"Change. It is unnerving to see."

"*It unnerves you? Let it unnerve you, you noble son-of-a-bitch!*" Clouds shredded with his cry.

Rifles cocked. The comte's hands flew into the air to stop the police's approach.

"No," Erik huffed, "let them come. Let them shoot. *Let them kill me.* I should have died as intended and never permitted your brother into my life!" Erik's laughter ripped apart what was left of the clouds. Raoul's brows raced up and his stance hardened. "You know so little of Erik. Fear *that*, Monsieur! Forget your wife's confessions and fear my history with the great Philippe de Chagny. If not for me listening to his lessons on compassion and redemption I would be dead and my daughter would never have been born, and she would not be dying right now and—"

"What rot are you speaking?"

"The rot I speak matters not when my daughter is dying, you nefarious fool!"

"This was an accident! A horrible tragedy—"

"That is right, Monsieur." He jerked his head in the direction Raoul looked. "Check and see how far away your guards are. *Erik* is unpredictable again." He clutched his roses and swaggered down the length of the hedgerow. "Now why would that be? Could poor unhappy Erik be that vengeful menace The *Phantom* right now because of the sins that are finally *yours*? Where is it? Where is your silver platter, so I can hand you my life on it. That is still what you want is it not? I let you go. I gave you Christine. I gave you my Opera House. I gave up my obsession with you. I gave you your life so many times I have lost count. I have never *wanted* to kill before, but I feel it in my marrow now. I want to kill *you*." Erik's head shot toward the sound of boots as the police marched forward. He pointed toward them.

"But yet again you win, because doing that will do nothing to ease my pain. So I stand here and try to decipher why you— of all people—came looking for me and I seek pity in my soul for your turmoil with your wife, but I have none. Finally, pity is not in the Phantom's vocabulary. The only one who deserves such is my daughter."

He pointed a shaking finger under Raoul's chin. His hand snaked up the length of his face. Like a boney spider's web, his skeletal fingers masked Raoul's expression. The comte instinctively turned his head, bringing Erik's hand with him and his lips inches from his ear.

"It may have been Loup's bullet, it may have been Legard's, but regardless, *your manhunt* pulled the trigger. Hand at the level of your eyes, Monsieur."

Erik shoved his face away and snapped his cloak, the sound ricocheting against air. He knocked Raoul aside with his shoulder, pleased a mask kept the tears of a father glistening privately in his eyes. He was more than willing for the world to see his wrath, but not his anguish.

Being a Phantom was far easier than being human.

Chapter Twenty

The doctors made rounds with their heads occasionally tipped together. Anna felt their eyes upon her each time they passed. Judging eyes and it was only due to the Comte de Chagny that they didn't turn a woman such as her out.

Her lip trembled. Her little miracle hadn't looked at her once or spoken since it happened. She just lay quietly in that bed never knowing the tears her mother shed. Anna was blinded by grief and it was a curse that she even saw the cup which appeared on the windowsill beside her.

"It's hot tea," a voice said softly.

Anna turned. The comtess stood behind her, her eyes cast down and to the side.

"My husband went in search of Erik this morning," she continued. "The Persian is keeping company with our sons and Simone."

"Vahid. His name is Vahid."

The comtess fidgeted. "I want to express my—"

"You can't have Erik, you know. Not in the way you wish him. All these years you've not wanted what you have, but wanted what love you *don't* have." Anna's opinion made the comtess wring her hands as if she were trying to grasp the idea.

"Do you remember when you first held your baby?" Anna asked abruptly.

"What mother doesn't?"

"Erik delivered Philippe. He was ecstatic he arrived and was perfect. He loves that boy so much." She covered her lips with the back of her hand. It pressed the salt of her tears against her mouth. Her words were muffled. "Have you ever seen Erik happy?"

The silence spoke enough.

She lowered her hand and raised her voice. "When we arrived in Germany and had Simone—I saw Erik ultimately happy."

The comtess kept her gaze downcast. Tears marred Anna's voice.

"Those early years on the run were so hard and utterly unnecessary. One confession by you could have put it all to rest. End this. I beg of you, end this manhunt now. Give that man one moment of peace and free us before our daughter— and his happiness—goes to God."

She hugged herself tightly, feeling choked by the pain of potentially never holding her baby again. Only one person could stem her agony.

"If you will excuse me, I need Erik." Anna bolted past her but stopped and turned back. "I am not your friend. I never will be. I don't want your tea or your apologies. I want you, for once, not to think of yourself."

* * * *

The confrontation in the Tuileries followed Raoul back to the hospital in Erik's wake as if it were chained to his leg. Erik's threats didn't frighten him. His humanity did. Raoul kept his strides steady as he forced himself through the halls.

Is Erik still a madman to me or merely a man? Why do I even wonder such? I must be tired. That's why I can't think clearly. That must be why I sympathize perhaps too much with him. I'm tired. Merely tired.

"Good morning, Father."

Raoul stopped short, nearly plowing into his son. Standing beside him was Philippe, looking drawn. Raoul nodded to his son but addressed Erik's.

"Your father, I take it, returned?"

The boy nodded. "He did. A few moments ago. He went to my sister. Monsieur le Comte—"

Philippe stopped and looked to André. His son nodded encouragingly. One would have to have been blind not to see the tentative alliance budding between the two.

Why is it children can so easily make amends? Raoul gestured with his gloves encouragingly to Philippe. "Go on."

"Do you wish me to ask?" André said.

Philippe shook his head. "No. She is my sister." He stepped forward and cleared his throat. "I know what I represent to you, Monsieur le Comte. I'm the son of a man you despise. I ask you set that aside. My...my father's history is not mine. I...I'm not him, and he would never think to do this, but I want to. That is, I would like to take my sister and—"

Philippe faltered. Raoul watched as the boy struggled to be a man as he scrubbed his eyes on his shirtsleeve. André squeezed his shoulder, shook it, and took over.

"If the doctors can do no more for her here, he wants to bring her to a quiet place to rest. She's different, father. Should she wake here, Philippe feels it would frighten her. Respectfully, can we move her to Chagny?"

Had his son gone mad?

"Absolutely not! I hear all the young man says, André, but—"

"Father, our physicians can tend her there until God decides whether she will live or—"

"Please, André, don't say it," Philippe whispered. "It is alright. He doesn't approve. Just leave it be. I am too tired to fight for..."

André stopped when Philippe bowed his head and looked away. It didn't make Raoul's choice any easier.

"André, to move that child is to move her family with her and I will not have Chagny disgraced by—"

"Your prejudices and obsessions?"

André boldly stepped forward and stood sideways between his father and Philippe. "*We* are not a disgrace, Father, for *we* have nothing to do with your history with the Phantom." André gestured between him and Philippe. "Your hostilities are perpetuated because you've not stopped *once* to let go of them. Chagny will be mine one day and it will be governed by the family creed you seem to ignore."

"Vicomte, not now!"

"Yes now." André pushed back with his words. "*Fidelity and compassion: the sacred endowments of our mind.* Where did your compassion go?" André pointed back to the ward. "There is a little girl in there dying—"

"André," Philippe whispered.

"No! I won't remain silent. You want this for her and you will have it, if only my father would see we no longer deserve to burden a past we did not create. If they want to live perpetuating their hatred, then let them. But I am Chagny as much as he is Chagny and the stigmas that are his are not mine. My uncle was able to find his compassion. So can I. The question is—can my father?"

When André faced him, Raoul wasn't looking at a boy anymore. He was looking at a man. *A man capable of holding the reins of Chagny far better than I ever did. A man I have been blind to.*

"Please, Father. He's my friend."

Chapter Twenty-One

The rose he clutched nearly snapped as he stormed down the halls. He ignored the nuns and doctors dodging his presence. He needed one person and one alone. Once Erik spied her, curled wearily in the Persian's care, his stance softened. Anna looked up at him with moon-sized eyes before bolting into his arms. She noticed the broken roses.

"Flowers?"

Erik had forgotten his precious gift and his heart sank. His perfect roses lay blemished in his hand. "For Simone. For when she—"

"Will you answer my questions, Erik, or shall I indeed keep my hand at the level of my eyes?"

Raoul's voice stabbed Erik in the back. He swallowed a growl and warned Vahid with a deadly gaze to keep him calm. The Persian rose.

"And what question is that, Monsieur?" Erik turned around. "If you want to know why your wife is still in love with me, riddle that of her and leave me be."

"No. It is regarding Philippe."

Anna looked up at Erik who was poised to spit venom when their sons appeared in the hall seconds behind Raoul.

"What of Uncle Philippe?" André inquired.

"What of me?" Philippe asked simultaneously.

Raoul gestured to the boy and addressed Erik. "I want to know why you named your son after my brother."

"Why?" The noise in Erik's head was blaringly loud.

"I have a decision to make and I must know."

Erik looked to the small woman in his arms and saw a flicker of confusion behind Anna's eyes. "It repulses me, Monsieur, that I am taking pause at this particular time of my family's grief to indulge you in your need for closure," he spat. "You and your brother were night and day. He was as irreproachable in conscience and compassion to me as you are in your lack of them. Oh the irony that each of you would hold a pillar in my particular part of hell."

"Get to your point. Time is of the essence."

"Your brother," Erik said forcefully, "faked my death and saved my life so to give me this." Broadly arching his arm he indicated everything around him. "Normalcy. The benefit of doubt! A life fitting in with any other life. An ordinary life, with ordinary people and ordinary problems with one brilliant exception! Extraordinary love. I named my son after him to remind myself that there is such a power as compassion. And in that, forgiveness." He handed Anna off to Vahid again.

"I can love, Monsieur, or does the cancer of my madness constantly cloak that imagery for you? What ordinary man would not be driven mad over what has happened because of your hunt? Do you think for one moment I actually would kill you and make good on my threats? That I would make you a priority over my daughter? Over my Anna? Over my Philippe? Leave off, Monsieur le Comte! Let my threats be just that—words spoken in anger. Words of a grieving and maddened mind. I am human! Let me chart my way through this part of hell like a normal man. Let me be alone and angry. Let me blame a God I don't believe in. Let me blame myself and let me grieve for my child. Let me be only in the company of those who love me for myself, *then* make your decision and do what you will with me. Time is not of the essence, for I have run out of it. I will do what I must for my family. Lock me away. Throw me in prison. Send me to my death if you will, but for now, let me be like anybody else—"

"Raoul?" Christine cut him off. As she rounded a corner and came into view, her hands were curled to her heart. "I thought I buried him once. Please, don't make me bury him again."

Erik pulled his eyes off of Raoul to study the quiver to her lips. Her voice shook drastically.

"This...this is killing him inside, can't you see?" She touched Raoul's shoulder. "Erik, you would die of a broken heart if not able to love that little girl wouldn't you? Yet you would sacrifice your life so she could live without this manhunt."

Erik looked to the Persian, then back to Christine. "I had said as much about dying of a broken heart years ago when you left me," he admitted evenly. "I intended to die and I would sacrifice everything to spare them this madness."

Christine shook her head. "Raoul, you lock him away and I will bury him no matter what. He will die of a broken heart not to be with her before you ever have a chance for justice to determine his fate. That little girl needs him to live."

Hesitantly Christine laid her hands on Erik's forearms. He flinched. He watched her eyes fill as she nodded to Anna as if some unspoken words were floating between them. She looked up and met his eyes.

"Forgive me. Please, Erik. Forgive me."

Christine sobbed as her knees gave out. Raoul reached forward to catch her but the Persian held him back. Erik had already done so and lowered her gently to the floor. She clutched the edge of his cloak.

"Please, Erik, forgive me for all I've done. You can't be locked away. If you sacrifice yourself for your family, who will teach Simone to love like you have taught me?" She turned and reached up to Raoul. "Please, Raoul, let them go. Please?" Christine looked at all the eyes upon her. "I beg all of you for forgiveness for perpetuating this with my jealousy and selfish intent. We must end this! For the sake of that little girl."

"Christine..." Erik came to one knee before her and placed his hands on her arms. Years ago such a touch would have sent him into a stupor of desperate want for her love. Her hands clutched the lapel of his coat as if she refused to let go. But she had to...

"I forgave all the moment my son was born. I even forgave myself my madness. I do not want you to beg for forgiveness. I would rather you not live your life in regret. I have made my choice in how to save my family from this madness. Do not plead on my behalf for anything otherwise. Let me live like anybody else. Anybody who loves would sacrifice all for their family."

He rose, leaving her staring up at him with eyes brimming in tears.

***

"Enough!" Raoul snapped. He took Christine's hand and drew her securely, but gently to his side. *Once I know the answer to one more question, I pray to have the same strength as my brother once did.* "I'm not speaking on any decisions over what to do regarding this manhunt, which will end as I see fit, but first answer my question." Raoul gritted his teeth. The last several hours had piled so much upon his shoulders it was a wonder he didn't fall. "Swearing upon the life of that little girl, answer truthfully: Did you or did you not kill my brother?"

For you will not set foot in my Chateau if you did, so help me God! I will burn alive for letting that innocent little girl down, but you will not enter Chagny if you so much as—

"I did not."

Raoul flinched. Erik spoke so quickly it was as if the words punched him in the gut. Erik stepped forward.

"You just displayed the difference between Philippe and yourself, Monsieur. He did not fear the truth or me as a man."

Raoul fought his tongue to keep it nailed to the floor of his mouth. He stared him down—eye to eye.

The truth? I will never know the truth and I am forced to take you at you word. For I keep... For a second his eyes ripped off of Erik and glanced in the direction of Simone's ward. *I keep thinking of the little girl and the daughter I lost. Thinking of what Philippe would do and I see you as a blasted father now and I cannot do this anymore. I cannot pretend you are not human to me.*

He ran his hand down his face until his moustache met his chin. "Any man who would swear against the life of his child must speak the truth." *I pray. I hope.* "My own heart feels that. I lost a child once because of this manhunt."

Arms akimbo, he stared heavenward and turned away. Turning, he jabbed a finger in the air between them. "If my brother were here today to see how children have suffered... This is over. I can endure it no more. I miss my baby girl. Still, after all these years and I cannot... I cannot see another suffer. Thank God for your daughter, Erik, for she did indeed just save your soul. We will see to it you are not pursued and that your life is returned to you as best as we can make it after all these years. Your son asked I move your daughter to the comfort of my Chateau where she can rest until God chooses her fate. *That* is the decision I had to make. And I thank God for my son for reminding me of how I was raised and who raised me. When God does choose...just go. Go...and never return! My brother gave you the benefit of doubt. I will give your freedom."

Anna's mouth gaped and she leaned on the Persian. Erik's eyes narrowed on them.

"What of Anna?" the Persian asked. "What of her fate?"

"She won't have to worry over Belgium if that is what you ask," Raoul's voice lowered. "In all these years I've never had contact with the duke who allegedly wants her. Not once. Loup was hungry for her—and he is dead." Raoul locked eyes with Erik.

"This manhunt ends?" Erik asked.

Raoul nodded and caught a glimpse of Philippe. The boy's head had tilted. It was as if he didn't comprehend.

"My answer to your request of me is yes," Raoul replied, speaking to him at last. "Go to your sister. I will speak to the doctors."

Unwillingly Raoul's eyes misted.

"You weep for my daughter?" Erik said incredulously.

"I weep for mine."

Chapter Twenty-Two

I wrote a madrigal. I composed an abendlied, but the most difficult piece to master has been my rondeau. The rondeau: recurrent themes between varied episodes used for the rapid final movement of a symphony... It is my life, is it not? All I ever wanted comes back to one theme: I want to live like anybody else. I believe I do now, and never has music been so familiar and so utterly—foreign. ~ Erik

A wind howled through the trees. A sound which for as long as Raoul could recall was associated with Chagny, as familiar as the ivy that crawled up its walls and the fog that blanketed the lands on warmer summer mornings. What were unfamiliar were the figures he spied though his library window, trudging across a light blanket of snow toward the Chagny crypts. The weeks that passed brought on that snow. Usually it muffled the world and made it clean and quiet. Raoul wished it could have muffled his thoughts.

"You are a million miles away."

He glanced to Christine. She had lowered her needlepoint and was studying the window as well.

"I've a million things on my mind," he replied.

"Like having Chagny back to normal?"

"Like having you back."

He reached to the server at his side and removed the stopper from a crystal decanter. He stared at the cognac filling his glass but didn't have the humor to drink. As soon as the carriage that stood loaded and waiting for its charges to depart Chagny left for good, would he breathe again.

Breathe, and start his life over.

The weeks had been long for both of them, but time had a way of slowly healing their wounds, of finding forgiveness and of starting over with each coming dawn. Each morning he began again with his wife, even with the presence of a Phantom, literally, among them. For the opportunity, Raoul was thankful. He only regretted that their healing conversations were spurred on at the bedside of little girl who never should have been there to begin with.

A knock scattered his thoughts. "Enter."

Raoul lowered the decanter as soon as he saw who it was and extended his hand. "Philippe." The lad bowed politely to his wife. He approached and shook Raoul's hand as if they were long friends. "I thought you would be readying to depart or—" he gestured out the window—"with your parents."

"No. I wished to remain behind, to take my leave of André and Monsieur Legard." He smiled at Christine. "Your wife and I already spent a long time in the music room together."

Raoul picked up his cognac and nodded. He shook the glass Philippe's way but the boy declined.

"These last three weeks have bonded you and our son in a way that reminds me much of my husband and his brother." Christine lifted her needle and hoop again, a smile on her face.

Raoul smiled back but didn't feel it reach his eyes. Yet it was the truth, he saw it too. "You regret leaving Chagny?" Raoul read certain sadness behind Philippe's eyes.

"I have found a sort of kindred spirit here, but my place is in Germany."

"Chagny will always be open to you," Christine assured. Raoul nodded.

"Thank you. You've been too kind. I know it has been awkward having us here." The silence told a story all its own. "And you, Monsieur le Comte, are an honorable man." Philippe reached into his pocket and withdrew a small slip of paper from L'Epoch. He laid the cutting down on the server. "True to your word, this manhunt is over?"

The glass was lowered until it covered the small clipping. Raoul lifted his eyes to Christine before he laid his hand on Philippe's shoulder and looked on him with fatherly eyes. "It is, and God willing may we all move beyond it. I..." Overcome, Raoul stopped. Only when Christine came to his side could he began again. "Son, I will never fully be amiable to your father. There are some things in life that will never be and some histories never meant to be forgotten. But I can live where we are now with them forgiven—as my brother did."

Philippe nodded and stood quietly beside them for a long while. "I...I should go. The carriage is waiting and we've a long trip back to Germany. Do...do you both mean it? Chagny will be open to me? I...will see André again? See...France and Paris again?"

Philippe extended his hand. Raoul noted a slight tremble to it. He took the hand only to draw the boy into his embrace.

"You have my word," he whispered into his ear.

As Philippe turned away to face the window, Raoul looked down and read the announcement on the clipping. He sighed when Christine reached across it and took his hand. He squeezed it. Curling her into his arms he turned them to the window as well, simply to remain by the boy's side as long as he stared across Chagny.

The Persian had done precisely as instructed. Raoul closed his eyes and prayed those words would once and for all bring closure to all of them.

Erik and Anna are dead.

* * * *

The wind blew the hem of Anna's skirt around her ankles making her draw the shawl tighter across her shoulders. The snow it grabbed danced in front of her before escaping on the breeze. Though she wanted to hasten to the carriage and be off and away from this foreign world of comfort and back to the seclusion of their monastery home, she let Erik take all the time he needed. For weeks he hadn't moved from the bedside of his child and now he needed this moment for himself. He knelt before the crypt, his head bowed to the ground.

"Are you all right?" she asked softly.

"I am tired, Anna."

"We will be home soon."

"*You* are my home." He struggled to his feet and laid a hand upon the name on the crypt.

"This is over, Erik. The comte was true to his word. We need not ever associate ourselves with Chagny. You are free."

"We will always be associated with it." Erik traced the name. "And we are never entirely free of our pasts. We need it to learn to shape our futures." He turned from the crypt and looked at her. Anna felt her cheeks warm. "Come." He extended one hand to her and the other out to his opposite side. "Let us take our future home."

Anna smiled through her tears as Simone, sitting quietly by her father's side took his hand and squealed as she was lifted high into his embrace. The violin she carried thumped lightly against his back as they walked away and toward the awaiting carriage. Her bandages still peeked out from beneath her dress but their presence didn't seem to dim her spirit.

"Papa!" She pointed back to the crypt with the bow.

Erik didn't turn. Anna stopped and looked behind her to where Simone pointed and for the first time tears of relief and peace ran down her face.

It was over. No more running. No more wondering if the past would haunt them. No more secrets between Chagny and a Phantom. Erik could live out his life like anybody else, but she knew.

He would never be like anybody else.

Erik would always be the Phantom and a madman. Redemptions and cures were all contrary to the truth. He wasn't a man to be reformed or healed. He was simply a man who, imprisoned by a black and malevolent madness, had a bright and supreme mind and a heart that could hold an empire. He just knew what he needed to control the noise and madness—patience and extraordinary love.

"You forgot your package," Simone scolded jabbing with the bow.

"I didn't forget. I've all the packages I need."

Anna smiled. Somehow she knew what he left at the base of Philippe's crypt.

Paper. Ink. Figs.

ABOUT THE AUTHOR

If one is going to query a publisher, Jennifer suggests not doing so in pink ink. Her first, written when she was twelve, was nothing if not colorful. She is a member of the Historical Novel Society and the Romance Writers of America in addition to being a writing mentor. Writing historical fiction and historical romance with unusual themes and locations, such as autism and the social mores of the mentally ill in the 19th century, she has a passion for Austrian culture and is often found searching for stories in long forgotten histories.

It was her love of research and classic literature that brought her to expanding Leroux's The Phantom of the Opera. Writing from a tiny loft office, Jennifer admits to being country mouse with city mouse tastes and is constantly fighting to keep the little critters in line. She can't pronounce pistachio, hates lollipops with gooey centers, and dearly loves to laugh.

Madrigal: A Novel of Gaston LeRoux's The Phantom of the Opera was the first book in the Madrigal series. *Abendlied* soon followed. *Rondeau* continues the haunting saga.

She enjoys hearing from her readers. E-mail her at author@jenniferlinforth.com

She can be found on the web at
www.jenniferlinforth.com

Praise for
Highland Press Books!

Rondeau - Jennifer Linforth has written a love story sure to please Phantom fans old and new alike.

~ Amanda Ashley, NYT Best-Selling Author

* * * *

I loved it! Curl up with three dashing, sexy pirates and three daring women in three delightful romances. **The Last Pirates** makes for great reading. You'll be wanting more from Cynthia Breeding—I know I will!

~ Sandra Madden, Best Selling Author

* * * *

Coming Home by Cynthia Owens - A heartwarming visit to a nineteenth century Irish village filled with memorable characters, post-famine intrigue, and bittersweet romance.

~ Pat McDermott, author of A Band of Roses

* * * *

If you want original medieval romance, captivating heroines, sexy heroes, stories of adventure, fantasy, and poignant love, Cynthia Breeding's **Lochs and Lasses** has it all!

~ Ann Major, USA Today Bestselling Author

* * * *

I enjoyed the wide vistas of Canadian scenery and the strong role of animals in the plot, especially the dogs and horses. **Passion and Prejudice** by Gail MacMillan is a thoroughly enjoyable read.

~ Sunflower, Long and Short Reviews

* * * *

Camelot's Enchantment by Cynthia Breeding is a highly original and captivating tale!

~ Joy Nash, USA Today Best Seller

* * * *

An anthology by amazing women with character and grace—incredible writers, wonderful stories! **For Your Heart Only** is not to be missed!

~ *Heather Graham, NYT Best Seller*

* * * *

Through its collection of descriptive phrases, **The Millennium Phrase Book** offers writers concrete examples of rich and evocative descriptions. Browsing through its pages offers a jumpstart to the imagination, helping authors deepen the intensity of scenes and enhance their own writing.

~ *Tami Cowden, Author of The Complete Guide to Heroes & Heroines, Sixteen Master Archetypes*

* * * *

Brynn Chapman makes you question how far science should take humanity. **Project Mendel** blurs the distinction between genetics and horror and merges them in a reality all too plausible. A gripping read.

~*Jennifer Linforth, Author, Historical Fiction and Romance*

* * * *

Abendlied: A Novel of Gaston LeRoux's The Phantom of the Opera – Madrigal continues. Jennifer Linforth has written another noteworthy tale about the Phantom. I enjoyed how the author takes the reader back to Erik's life below the opera house to unfold a new tale with the Phantom's friendship with Comte Philippe de Chagny. This is the second book in the series. It does stand alone, but I believe the reader may take pleasure reading Madrigal first to thoroughly enjoy the continued tale of The Phantom of the Opera.

~*Karen Michelle Nutt, PRN Reviews*

* * * *

Kemberlee Shortland's **A Piece of My Heart** is terrific romantic/suspense fiction to savor and share with family and friends.

~*Viviane Crystal, Crystal Reviews*

* * * *

From betrayal, to broken hearts, to finding love again, **Second Time Around** has a story for just about anyone. these fine ladies created stories that will always stay fresh in my heart; ones I will treasure forever.

~ *Cherokee , Coffee Time Romance & More*

* * * *

The Mosquito Tapes - Nobody tells a bio-terror story better than Chris Holmes. Just nobody. And like all of Chris Holmes' books, this one begins well—when San Diego County Chief Medical Examiner Jack Youngblood discovers a strange mosquito in the pocket of a murder victim Taut, tingly, and downright scary, *The Mosquito Tapes* will keep you reading well into the night. But best be wary: Spray yourself with Deet and have a fly swatter nearby.

~ Ben F. Small, author of Alibi On Ice and The Olive Horseshoe

* * * *

Cynthia Breeding's ***Prelude to Camelot*** is a lovely and fascinating read, a book worthy of being shelved with my Arthuriana fiction and non-fiction.

~ Brenda Thatcher, Mystique Books

* * * *

Romance on Route 66 by Judith Leigh and Cheryl Norman – Norman and Leigh break the romance speed limit on America's historic roadway.

~ Anne Krist, Ecataromance, Reviewers' Choice Award Winner

* * * *

Ah, the memories that ***Operation: L.O.V.E.*** brings to mind. As an Air Force nurse who married an Air Force fighter pilot, I relived the days of glory through each and every story. While covering all the military branches, each story holds a special spark of its own that readers will love!

~ Lori Avocato, Best Selling Author

* * * *

In ***Fate of Camelot***, Cynthia Breeding develops the Arthur-Lancelot-Gwenhwyfar relationship. In many Arthurian tales, Guinevere is a rather flat character. Cynthia Breeding gives her a depth of character as the reader sees her love for Lancelot and her devotion to the realm as its queen. The reader feels the pull she experiences between both men. In addition, the reader feels more of the deep friendship between Arthur and Lancelot seen in Malory's Arthurian tales. In this area, Cynthia Breeding is more faithful to the medieval Arthurian tradition than a glamorized Hollywood version. She does not gloss over the difficulties of Gwenhwyfar's role as queen and as woman, but rather develops them to give the reader a vision of a woman who lives her role as queen and lover with all that she is.

~ Merri, Merrimon Books

* * * *

Rape of the Soul - Ms. Thompson's characters are unforgettable. Deep, promising and suspenseful this story was. I couldn't put it down. Around every corner was something that you didn't know was going to happen. If you love a sense of history in a book, then I suggest reading this book!

~ Ruth Schaller, Paranormal Romance Reviews

Jennifer Linforth

* * * *

Static Resistance and Rose – An enticing, fresh voice. Lee Roland knows how to capture your heart.

~ Kelley St. John, National Readers Choice Award Winner

* * * *

Southern Fried Trouble - Katherine Deauxville is at the top of her form with mayhem, sizzle and murder.

~ Nan Ryan, NY Times Best-Selling Author

* * * *

Madrigal: A Novel of Gaston LeRoux's The Phantom of the Opera - Ms. Linforth has written a love story sure to please Phantom fans old and new alike.

~ Amanda Ashley, NYT Best-selling author

* * * *

Cave of Terror by Amber Dawn Bell - Highly entertaining and fun, ***Cave of Terror*** was impossible to put down. Though at times dark and evil, Ms. Bell never failed to inject some light-hearted humor into the story. Delightfully funny with a true sense of teenagers, Cheyenne is believable and her emotional struggles are on par with most teens. The author gave just enough background to understand the workings of her vampires. I truly enjoyed Ryan and Constantine. Ryan was adorable and a teenager's dream. Constantine was deliciously dark. Ms. Bell has done an admirable job of telling a story suitable for young adults.

~ Dawnie, Fallen Angel Reviews

* * * *

The Sense of Honor - Ashley Kath-Bilsky has written a historical romance of the highest caliber. This reviewer fell in love with the hero and was cheering for the heroine all the way through. The plot is exciting, characters are multi-dimensional, and the secondary characters bring life to the story. Sexual tension rages through this story and Ms. Kath-Bilsky gives her readers a breathtaking romance. The love scenes are sensual and very romantic. This reviewer was very pleased with how the author handled all the secrets and both characters reacted very maturely when the secrets finally came to light.

~ Valerie, Love Romances and More

* * * *

Highland Wishes by Leanne Burroughs. The storyline, set in a time when tension was high between England and Scotland, is a fast-paced tale. The reader can feel this author's love for Scotland and its many wonderful heroes. This reviewer was easily captivated by the story and was enthralled by it until the end. The reader will laugh and cry as you read this wonderful story. The reader feels all the pain, torment and disillusionment felt by both main characters, but also the joy and love they felt. Ms. Burroughs has crafted a well-researched story that gives a glimpse into Scotland during a time when there was upheaval and war for independence. This reviewer commends her for a wonderful job done.

~Dawn Roberto, Love Romances

* * * *

I adore this Scottish historical romance! ***Blood on the Tartan*** has more history than some historical romances—but never dry history! Readers will find themselves completely immersed in the scene, the history and the characters. Chris Holmes creates a multi-dimensional theme of justice in his depiction of all the nuances and forces at work from the laird down to the land tenants. This intricate historical detail emanates from the story itself, heightening the suspense and the reader's understanding of the history in a vivid manner as if it were current and present. The extra historical detail just makes their life stories more memorable and lasting because the emotions were grounded in events. ***Blood On The Tartan*** is a must read for romance and historical fiction lovers of Scottish heritage.

~Merri, Merrimon Reviews

* * * *

Chasing Byron by Molly Zenk is a page turner of a book not only because of the engaging characters, but also by the lovely prose. Reading this book was a jolly fun time all through the eyes of Miss Woodhouse, yet also one that touches the heart. It was an experience I would definitely repeat. Ms. Zenk must have had a glorious time penning this story.

~Orange Blossom, Long and Short Reviews

* * * *

Moon of the Falling Leaves is an incredible read. The characters are not only believable, but the blending in of how Swift Eagle shows Jessica and her children the acts of survival is remarkably done. Diane Davis White pens a poignant tale that really grabbed this reader. She tells a descriptive story of discipline, trust and love in a time where hatred and prejudice abounded among many. This rich tale offers vivid imagery of the beautiful scenery and landscape, and brings in the tribal customs of each person, as Jessica and Swift Eagle search their heart.

~Cherokee, Coffee Time Romance

Jennifer Linforth

* * * *

Jean Harrington's *The Barefoot Queen* is a superb historical with a lushly painted setting. I adored Grace for her courage and the cleverness with which she sets out to make Owen see her love for him. The bond between Grace and Owen is tenderly portrayed and their love had me rooting for them right up until the last page. Ms. Harrington's *The Barefoot Queen* is a treasure in the historical romance genre you'll want to read for yourself! Five Star Pick of the Week!!!

~ *Crave More Romance*

* * * *

Almost Taken by Isabel Mere takes the reader on an exciting adventure. The compelling characters of Deran Morissey, the Earl of Atherton, and Ava Fychon, a young woman from Wales, find themselves drawn together as they search for her missing siblings.

Readers will watch in interest as they fall in love and overcome obstacles.

This is a sensual romance, and a creative and fast moving storyline that will enthrall readers. Ava, who is highly spirited and stubborn, will win the respect of the readers for her courage and determination. Deran, who is rumored in the beginning to be an ice king, not caring about anyone, will prove how wrong people's perceptions can be. *Almost Taken* is an emotionally moving historical romance that I highly recommend.

~ *Anita, The Romance Studio*

* * * *

Leanne Burroughs easily will captivate the reader with intricate details, a mystery that ensnares the reader and characters that will touch their hearts. By the end of the first chapter, this reviewer was enthralled with *Her Highland Rogue* and was rooting for Duncan and Catherine to admit their love. Laughter, tears and love shine through this wonderful novel. This reviewer was amazed at Ms. Burroughs' depth and perception in this storyline. Her wonderful way with words plays itself through each page like a lyrical note and will captivate the reader till the very end.

Read *Her Highland Rogue* and be transported to a time full of mystery and promise of a future. This reviewer is highly recommending this book for those who enjoy an engrossing Scottish tale full of humor, love and laughter.

~*Dawn Roberto, Love Romances*

* * * *

Bride of Blackbeard by Brynn Chapman is a compelling tale of sorrow, pain, love, and hate. From the moment I started reading about Constanza and her upbringing, I was torn. Each of the people she encounters on her journey has an experience to share, drawing in the reader more. Ms. Chapman sketches a story that tugs at the heartstrings. I believe many will be touched in some way by this extraordinary book that leaves much thought.

~ *Cherokee, Coffee Time Romance*

* * * *

Isabel Mere's skill with words and the turn of a phrase makes *Almost Guilty* a joy to read. Her characters reach out and pull the reader into the trials, tribulations, simple pleasures, and sensual joy that they enjoy.

Ms. Mere unravels the tangled web of murder, smuggling, kidnapping, hatred and faithless friends, while weaving a web of caring, sensual love that leaves a special joy and hope in the reader's heart.

~ *Camellia, Long and Short Reviews*

* * * *

Beats A Wild Heart - In the ancient, Celtic land of Cornwall, Emma Hayward searched for a myth and found truth. The legend of the black cat of Bodmin Moor is a well known Cornish legend. Jean Adams has merged the essence of myth and romance into a fascinating story which catches the imagination. I enjoyed the way the story unfolded at a smooth and steady pace with Emma and Seth appearing as real people who feel an instant attraction for one another. At first the story appears to be straightforward, but as it evolves mystery, love and intrigue intervene to make a vibrant story with hidden depths. Once you start reading you won't be able to put this book down.

~ *Orchid, Long and Short Reviews*

* * * *

Down Home Ever Lovin' Mule **Blues** by Jacquie Rogers - How can true love fail when everyone and their mule, cat, and skunk know that Brody and Rita belong together, even if Rita is engaged to another man?

Needless to say, this is a fabulous roll on the floor while laughing out loud story. I am so thrilled to discover this book, and the author who wrote it. Rarely do I locate a story with as much humor, joy, and downright lust spread so thickly on the pages that I am surprised I could turn the pages. A treasure not to be missed.

~*Suziq2, Single Titles.com*

* * * *

Saving Tampa - What if you knew something horrible was going to happen but you could prevent it? Would you tell someone? What if you saw it in a vision and had no proof? Would you risk your credibility to come forward? These are the questions at the heart of *Saving Tampa*, an on-the-edge-of-your-seat thriller from Jo Webnar, who has written a wonderful suspense that is as timely as it is entertaining.

~ Mairead Walpole, Reviews by Crystal

* * * *

In the Lion's Mouth by Jean Harrington - Impressive! Harrington delights with an evocative tale sure to please. A strong heroine, intense emotion, and a vivid setting make **In The Lion's Mouth** a breathtaking romance. Well done!

~ Sue-Ellen Welfonder, USA Today Bestselling Author

* * * *

When the Vow Breaks by Judith Leigh - This book is about a woman who fights breast cancer. I assumed it would be extremely emotional and hard to read, but it was not. The storyline dealt more with the commitment between a man and a woman, with a true belief of God.

The intrigue was that of finding a rock to lean upon through faith in God. Not only did she learn to lean on her relationship with Him, but she also learned how to forgive her husband. This is a great look at not only a breast cancer survivor, but also a couple whose commitment to each other through their faith grew stronger. It is an easy read and one I highly recommend.

~ Brenda Talley, The Romance Studio

* * * *

A Heated Romance by Candace Gold - A fascinating romantic suspense tells the story of Marcie O'Dwyer, a female firefighter who has had to struggle to prove herself. While the first part of the book seems to focus on the romance and Marcie's daily life, the second part transitions into a suspense novel as Marcie witnesses something suspicious at one of the fires. Her life is endangered by what she possibly knows and I found myself anticipating the outcome almost as much as Marcie.

~ Lilac, Long and Short Reviews

* * * *

Into the Woods by R.R. Smythe - This Young Adult Fantasy will send chills down your spine. I, as the reader, followed Callum and witnessed everything he and his friends went through as they attempted to decipher the messages. At the same time, I watched Callum's mother, Ellsbeth, as she walked through the Netherwood. Each time Callum deciphered one of the four messages, some villagers awakened. Through the eyes of Ellsbeth, I saw the other sleepers wander, make mistakes, and be released from the Netherwood, leaving Ellsbeth alone. Excellent reading for any age of fantasy fans!

~ Detra Fitch, Huntress Reviews

Rondeau

＊ ＊ ＊ ＊

Like the Lion, the Witch, and the Wardrobe, ***Dark Well of Decision*** is a grand adventure with a likable girl who is a little like all of us. Zoe's insecurities are realistically drawn and her struggle with both her faith and the new direction her life will take is poignant. The references to the Bible and the teachings presented are appropriately captured. Author Anne Kimberly is an author to watch; her gift for penning a grand childhood adventure is a great one. This one is well worth the time and money spent.

~Lettetia, Coffee Time Romance

＊ ＊ ＊ ＊

The Crystal Heart by Katherine Deauxville brims with ribald humor and authentic historical detail. Enjoy!

~ Virginia Henley, NY Times bestselling author

＊ ＊ ＊ ＊

In Sunshine or In Shadow by Cynthia Owens - If you adore the stormy heroes of 'Wuthering Heights' and 'Jane Eyre' (and who doesn't?) you'll be entranced by Owens' passionate story of Ireland after the Great Famine, and David Burke - a man from America with a hidden past and a secret name. Only one woman, the fiery, luscious Siobhan, can unlock the bonds that imprison him. Highly recommended for those who love classic romance and an action-packed story.

~ Best Selling Author, Maggie Davis, AKA Katherine Deauxville

＊ ＊ ＊ ＊

Rebel Heart - Jannine Corti Petska used a myriad of emotions to tell this story and the reader quickly becomes entranced in the ways Courtney's stubborn attitude works to her advantage in surviving this disastrous beginning to her new life. This is a wonderful rendition of a different type which is a welcome addition to the historical romance genre. I believe that you will enjoy this story; I know I did!

~ Brenda Talley, The Romance Studio

＊ ＊ ＊ ＊

Brides of the West by Michèle Ann Young, Kimberly Ivey, and Billie Warren Chai - All three of the stories in this wonderful anthology are based on women who gambled their future in blindly accepting complete strangers for husbands. It was a different era when a woman must have a husband to survive and all three of these phenomenal authors wrote exceptional stories featuring fascinating and gutsy heroines and the men who loved them. For an engrossing read with splendid original stories I highly encourage readers to pick up a copy of this marvelous anthology.

~ Marilyn Rondeau, Reviewers International Organization

* * * *

Cat O'Nine Tales by Deborah MacGillivray. Enchanting tales from the most wicked, award-winning author today. Spellbinding! A treat for all.

~ *Detra Fitch, Huntress Reviews*

* * * *

Faery Special Romances - Brilliantly magical! Jacquie Rogers' special brand of humor and imagination will have you believing in faeries from page one. Absolutely enchanting!

~ *Dawn Thompson, Award Winning Author*

* * * *

Flames of Gold *(Anthology)* - Within every heart lies a flame of hope, a dream of true love, a glimmering thought that the goodness of life is far, far larger than the challenges and adversities arriving in every life. In ***Flames of Gold*** lie five short stories wrapping credible characters into that mysterious, poignant mixture of pain and pleasure, sorrow and joy, stony apathy and resurrected hope.

Deftly plotted, paced precisely to hold interest and delightfully unfolding, ***Flames of Gold*** deserves to be enjoyed in any season, guaranteeing that real holiday spirit endures within the gifts of faith, hope and love personified in these engaging, spirited stories!

~ *Viviane Crystal, Crystal Reviews*

* * * *

Romance Upon A Midnight Clear *(Anthology)* - Each of these stories is well-written; when grouped together, they pack a powerful punch. Each author shares exceptional characters and a multitude of emotions ranging from grief to elation. You cannot help being able to relate to these stories that touch your heart and will entertain you at any time of year, not just the holidays. I feel honored to have been able to sample the works of such talented authors.

~*Matilda, Coffee Time Romance*

* * * *

Christmas is a magical time and twelve talented authors answer the question of what happens when ***Christmas Wishes*** come true in this incredible anthology. Each of these highly skilled authors brings a slightly different perspective to the Christmas theme to create a book that is sure to leave readers satisfied. What a joy to read such splendid stories! This reviewer looks forward to more anthologies by Highland Press as the quality is simply astonishing.

Rondeau

~ *Debbie, CK2S Kwips and Kritiques*

* * * *

Recipe for Love *(Anthology)* - I don't think the reader will find a better compilation of mouth watering short romantic love stories than in ***Recipe for Love***! This is a highly recommended volume–perfect for beaches, doctor's offices, or anywhere you've a few minutes to read.

~ *Marilyn Rondeau, Reviewers International Organization*

* * * *

Holiday in the Heart *(Anthology)* - Twelve stories that would put even Scrooge into the Christmas spirit. It does not matter what *type* of romance genre you prefer. This book has a little bit of everything. The stories are set in the U.S.A. and Europe. Some take place in the past, some in the present, and one story takes place in both! I strongly suggest you put on something comfortable, brew up something hot (tea, coffee or cocoa will do), light up a fire, settle down somewhere quiet and begin reading this anthology.

~ *Detra Fitch, Huntress Reviews*

* * * *

Blue Moon Magic is an enchanting collection of short stories. It offers historicals, contemporaries, time travel, paranormal, and futuristic narratives to tempt your heart.

Legend says that if you wish with all your heart upon the rare blue moon, your wishes were sure to come true. In some of the stories, love happens in the most unusual ways. Angels may help, ancient spells may be broken. Even vampires will find their perfect mate with the power of the blue moon.

Blue Moon Magic is a perfect read for late at night or during your commute to work. The short yet sweet stories are a wonderful way to spend a few minutes. If you do not have the time to finish a full-length novel, and hate stopping in the middle of a loving tale, I highly recommend grabbing this book.

~ *Kim Swiderski, Writers Unlimited Reviewer*

* * * *

Legend has it that a blue moon is enchanted. What happens when fifteen talented authors utilize this theme to create enthralling stories of love? Readers will find a wide variety of time periods and styles showcased in this superb anthology. ***Blue Moon Enchantment*** is sure to offer a little bit of something for everyone!

~ *Debbie, CK²S Kwips and Kritiques*

Jennifer Linforth

* * * *

Love Under the Mistletoe is a fun anthology that infuses the beauty of the season with fun characters and unforgettable situations. This is one of those books you can read year round and still derive great pleasure from each of the charming stories. A wonderful compilation of holiday stories.

~ *Chrissy Dionne, Romance Junkies*

* * * *

Love and Silver Bells - I really enjoyed this heart-warming anthology. The characters are heart-wrenchingly human and hurting and simply looking for a little bit of peace on earth. Luckily they all eventually find it, although not without some strife. But we always appreciate the gifts we receive when we have to work a little harder to keep them. I recommend these warm holiday tales be read by the light of a well-lit tree, with a lovely fire in the fireplace and a nice cup of hot cocoa. All will warm you through and through.
~ *Angi, Night Owl Romance*

* * * *

Love on a Harley is an amazing romantic anthology featuring six amazing stories. Each story was heartwarming, tear jerking, and so perfect. I got tied to each one wanting them to continue on forever. Lost love, rekindling love, and learning to love are all expressed within these pages beautifully. I couldn't ask for a better romance anthology; each author brings that sensual, longing sort of love that every woman dreams of. Great job ladies!

~ *Crystal, Crystal Book Reviews*

* * * *

No Law Against Love *(Anthology)* - If you have ever found yourself rolling your eyes at some of the more stupid laws, then you are going to adore this novel. Twenty-four stories fill this anthology, each dealing with at least one stupid or outdated law. Let me give you an example: In Florida, USA, there is a law that states 'If an elephant is left tied to a parking meter, the parking fee has to be paid just as it would for a vehicle.' Yes, you read that correctly. No matter how many times you go back and reread them, the words will remain the same. The tales take place in the present, in the past, in the USA, in England . . . in other words, there is something for everyone! Best yet, profits from the sales of this novel will go to breast cancer prevention.

A stellar anthology that had me laughing, sighing in pleasure, believing in magic, and left me begging for more! This is one novel that will go directly to my 'Keeper' shelf, to be read over and over again. Very highly recommended!

~ *Detra Fitch, Huntress Reviews*
(This hilarious book is now out-of-print, but copies are still available through our website or from Amazon. A revised edition is at Kindle)

* * * *

172

Rondeau

No Law Against Love 2 - I'm sure you've heard about some of those silly laws, right? Well, this anthology, with the continuation of the silly laws theme, shows us that sometimes those silly laws can bring just the right people together.

I highly recommend this anthology. Each story is a gem and each author has certainly given their readers value for money.

~ *Valerie, Love Romances and More*

Be sure to check our website often

http://highlandpress.org

CPSIA information can be obtained at www.ICGtesting.com
Printed in the USA
LVOW041030091211

258616LV00001B/42/P